BESTSELLING AUTHOR OF THE *RUGBY SPIRIT* SERIES

GERARD SIGGINS

FOOTBALL FIESTA

THE O'BRIEN PRESS
DUBLIN

This edition first published 2019 by
The O'Brien Press Ltd,
12 Terenure Road East, Rathgar,
Dublin 6, D06 HD27 Ireland.
Originally published in 2018 as *Sports Academy: Atlantis United*

Tel: +353 1 4923333; Fax: +353 1 4922777
E-mail: books@obrien.ie.
Website: www.obrien.ie

The O'Brien Press is a member of Publishing Ireland
ISBN: 978-1-78849-095-5
Text © copyright Gerard Siggins 2018

1 3 5 7 8 6 4 2

19 21 23 22 20

Printed and bound by CPI Group (UK) Ltd, Croydon, CR0 4YY.
The paper in this book is produced using pulp from managed forests.

Published in

DUBLIN
UNESCO
City of Literature

DEDICATION

To Sadhbh, John, Anna, Caitlin, Emma-Dee and Tilly
– future stars at Atlantis Academy

Acknowledgements

Thanks, as always, to Martha, Jack, Lucy and Billy,
and forever to Mam and Dad.
Thanks also to the excellent O'Brien Press publishing team,
especially my editor, Helen Carr.
I've spent a lot of time watching sport everywhere from
public parks to Olympic stadiums – thanks to all the
players and coaches whose efforts give me such pleasure.

CHAPTER 1

Joe kicked the ground in frustration. It was the first thing he had kicked all afternoon.

Joe played left-back on his team, Woodstock Wanderers, but nobody ever passed the ball to him. It wasn't that he was unpopular, just that his team-mates knew that he was likely to lose possession as soon as they gave him the ball.

'You've got two left feet, Joe,' chuckled the coach as they walked off at half-time. Joe wished he *did* have two left feet – as that was the one he actually kicked with. The coach had obviously not noticed because Joe had so few chances to kick the ball.

'Two right feet, you mean,' sniffed Joe.

The coach chuckled again. 'Sorry, Joe….'

Just twice in the first half Joe had seen the ball up close – each time as the opposition winger had nipped past him. His belated attempt at a tackle missed the player by half a metre.

Luckily, neither of these breaks cost his team a goal, and

Woodstock were leading 1-0 at the break.

'Nice goal, Robbie,' Joe told the team's star player, who played centre forward.

'Thanks, Joe,' Robbie grinned back.

'Did you see that guy on the far side,' asked Jakob, pointing at a man wearing a long, padded coat that covered his shins, a thick scarf wrapped several times around his neck, and a stylish black hat. 'He looks like a scout – maybe he's from United?'

The boys all turned and stared at the mysterious stranger, who looked nothing like the rest of the spectators – mostly their mums and dads – dressed in anoraks and woolly beanies.

'He's obviously here to have a look at you,' one of the boys blurted, pointing at Robbie.

The striker grinned and shrugged his shoulders. There was no point being modest. He wasn't cocky about it at all, but he – and everyone else – knew he was the best player on the team. By far.

Robbie went on to prove that beyond doubt early in the second half with two excellent goals, one a diving header from a corner.

Joe, meanwhile, managed to execute one successful tackle – although the ball ran away for a throw-in – and also gathered a loose ball which he kicked as far as he could up-field.

He was happy with that contribution, and thought to himself how relieved he was that neither of the opposition's goals were his fault.

But disaster struck with just one minute left on the clock. The Woodstock centre back was hurried into clearing the ball, and a powerful header from midfield propelled the ball all the way back so it bounced into Joe's path. All he had to do was kick it back from where it had come, but in his excitement he took a wild swing at the ball – and slipped.

As his standing leg went from under him, the opposition winger dodged out of the way and collected the ball as it bounced away towards the goal.

Joe was still on his hands and knees in the sticky mud when the winger's shot hit the back of the net. The referee thrust his arm in the air and blew his whistle to signal the goal, and immediately gave two more long blasts of the whistle to denote the end of the game and a 3-3 draw.

Joe's head dropped, but he struggled to his feet and turned to find the quickest route to the dressing room. He stopped to shake the hands of the opposition players he met, but was more concerned with the battle with his own tear ducts, which wanted to run free. Crying would be just too humiliating for him after costing his team two precious league points.

None of his team-mates would look him in the eye as they wandered off, except Robbie, who sought him out to put an arm across his shoulder, congratulate him on a pretty good game, and tell him not to worry about what happened at the end.

In the dressing room Joe changed quickly, keen to get out of there with as little delay as possible. He zipped up his hoodie and slung his bag over his shoulder, muttering a 'see you Tuesday' to the boy next to him before heading for the door.

At that moment, the coach's large frame filled the doorway. He stared down at Joe with a puzzled look on his face.

'Ah... Joe... Can you hang on for a minute, I need to talk to you with your parents.'

Joe's face fell, and his insides felt as if someone had kicked him. His team-mates stared across at him, but no one wanted to meet his eyes.

The coach gave his post-match talk to the boys, but he was clearly distracted by something. Not that Joe noticed, as his mind raced about what the coach was going to say. He was obviously going to drop him, maybe even ask him to leave the club.

The coach finished up and told the team to make sure to be on time for training on Tuesday. He nodded at Joe and signalled for him to go outside.

The parents were milling around, full of chat about the game and their plans for the weekend ahead. Joe's mum gave him a sympathetic look, and his dad put his hand on his shoulder. 'Hard luck, Joe, you were very unlucky at the end there,' he smiled.

Joe smiled awkwardly back, but his gaze was fixed on the door to the changing rooms. Out strode the coach, who made straight for the trio.

'Joe, Mr Wright, Mrs Wright, can you come with me, I've someone who wants to talk to you. He says his name is Fry,' as he led them away from the gathering of parents and into the car park.

At the end of the line of cars a man was sucking on a cigarette, the smoke drifting into the sky. But Joe didn't notice that, because he was fixed on what the man wore on his head – a stylish black hat.

CHAPTER 2

Kim was having a bad day too. She had only taken up rugby the year before, but already she loved it and lived for the training and games with her club, Seaside Spartans. She liked the way everyone had their role, and all shapes and sizes could fit in, and playing in the backs gave her a chance to run with the ball.

But while she enjoyed the excitement of taking the ball under her arm and sidestepping opponents before charging into space, other aspects of her game needed work. She was one of the weakest members of the team, and the coach never tired of pointing that out.

'You couldn't tackle your way out of a wet paper bag,' growled the coach as Kim tumbled into touch while the opposition winger charged up the touchline to score.

Kim hated when the coach was negative – and not just about her.

'I didn't do it on purpose,' she muttered to herself. Her friend, Amy, helped her up and the pair jogged back while the kicker readied herself for the conversion.

'I hate when coach singles players out,' agreed Amy. 'I wish we had a different coach. I'm thinking of giving up.'

'Oh, please don't!' replied Kim. 'Just ignore his insults and concentrate on getting better. I've never enjoyed a sport as much as this and I want to stick with it.'

The Spartans played their home games in the girls' school grounds, and some of the teachers came along to support them.

'Hard luck, Kim,' called out Miss Conlon, everyone's favourite Geography teacher. 'You'll get there, don't worry.'

Kim smiled and waved back at the teacher who was standing beside a short, dark woman carrying a clipboard.

She knew she had a problem with her tackling technique. She had even studied all the best players in slow motion on YouTube, but when confronted with an opponent in real life all her plans seemed to fall apart.

It was a cold, wet day and there were few chances for anyone to try out their speedy running, however. The game developed into a gritty forward battle with the ball invisible to most spectators – and even players – under a succession of scrums, rucks and mauls.

The coach made a series of substitutions and Kim was moved to full-back where she suddenly felt very vulnerable. She had to concentrate on every play and anticipate what it might mean to her.

There wasn't much time left in the game when she suddenly realised she was about to take centre stage.

The opposition out-half unleashed a long, low kick into the corner, more than thirty metres from Kim. It was obviously a pre-worked move as the speedy winger was already hurtling towards the ball.

Kim reckoned she was as quick as her opponent, but she had a lot of ground to make up so she slightly changed direction – abandoning getting to the ball first, but giving her a better chance of stopping the winger.

She gambled correctly, and was still moving at top speed when she crashed into her opponent's thigh. There was a huge cheer from the Spartans' support, but it didn't last very long as the winger flipped the ball back over her shoulder. The opposition centre was following in support and easily ran in under the posts.

'Kim!' roared the coach, his face turning purple. 'You should have hit her harder and buried her in touch.'

Kim sank to the ground, breathless and soul-destroyed.

'Rubbish,' came a voice. 'She made the right call to switch focus and hit the winger, and that pass for the try was a total fluke.'

Kim looked up, wondering who had dared to contradict the coach. She saw him turning a deeper purple as he turned to see the woman with the clipboard who had been standing with Miss Conlon.

'Who are you to say that?' he sneered.

'Rugby coach level 4,' she replied, coolly.

The Spartans' coach turned away, trying to keep his anger under wraps.

After the conversion was taken, the referee blew the whistle on a 10-0 defeat for Spartans and Amy and Kim trudged unhappily back to the shed in which they changed. The coach gave them a thirty-second telling off, but everyone could see he had been rattled by the comment from the sideline.

'I really enjoyed that,' chuckled Amy. 'It's good to see him getting a taste of his own medicine.'

Miss Conlon tapped on the door of the shed, and stuck her head inside.

'Hard luck, Spartans, but there was loads there to encourage us. I think you'll be winning trophies next season if you keep working.'

The teacher's friend joined her. 'Hi, I'm Kelly. I just want to say that I've apologised to your coach because although he was wrong, what I said was out of order. I coach some very senior rugby players and I saw plenty of talent here today, so keep working at it.'

Kelly turned and left, but just as Miss Conlon went to join her, she pointed at Kim.

'Yes, you, Kim. Can you join us outside? Kelly wants to have a word with you.'

CHAPTER 3

Craig used to like bagels, but now he dreaded every mention of the chewy, O-shaped bread roll. He liked tennis even more than bagels, although his results this indoor season left a lot to be desired.

'6-0, 6-0, another double bagel,' sighed the coach of his club's Under 12 side. 'That's four matches in a row you haven't won a single game.'

Craig shrugged his shoulders. He had worked so hard at getting better, smashing a ball against a wall all afternoon to get his eye in, but he always seemed to freeze when it came to competitive matches.

There were only four under-12 players in Shelbourne LTC, so Craig didn't have to worry about losing his place, but he was seriously considering just pulling out as the humiliating defeats piled up.

There was a reverse singles round to come, and then a game of doubles, and Craig decided that if he didn't win another game he would tell his team-mates he had enough.

He joined Andy knocking up on the outside court, wrapped up warm against the chilly air where they had to get used to the weaker light cast by the floodlights.

'You've a really strong forehand,' his team-mate called out. 'I don't understand why you don't win more games.'

Craig just shrugged his shoulders. He had tried to analyse why he made mistakes, but in the end he decided it wasn't a technical issue, just that he always seemed to freeze when the pressure of competition came on. He had heard TV commentators talking about tennis players and golfers who 'choke' at crucial moments and recognised himself, but the more he tried to fight it the worse he got.

He and Andy smashed balls back at each other for a few minutes longer before they got the signal from their coach that they were needed back inside.

Craig wiped the handle of his racket in a towel and cast his eyes around the large sports hall. It was almost empty – his mother and sister always came along to support him, but the total attendance was still in single figures. He knew them all, or at least he had during the earlier game. Since he had been outside, another spectator had arrived, and as he was wearing a bright turquoise tracksuit it was hard to avoid him.

Craig studied the new arrival – he was sure he'd never seen him before and it was unlikely he was with the opposing team as they were staring and pointing at him just as much as the Shelbourne boys were.

The referee called them all to order and Craig's reverse singles contest began. He was up against a weaker opponent than earlier, but still he couldn't get things right. He heeded Andy's compliment about his forehand, and tried to use it as much as possible, but he seemed to try too hard and over-hit the ball out of play.

As he mopped his brow at one of the changeovers, his gaze caught the eye of the man in the loud tracksuit, who was staring intensely at him. Craig was a bit rattled by that and, struggling to concentrate, lost the next game in a rush. Soon, the first set was lost 6-0.

His sister called out some words of encouragement, and it seemed to snap Craig out of his confused and distracted state. He started to focus more on each shot, and soon won a few points. His opponent had been laughing and joking with his team-mates between sets, and Craig's new drive seemed to rattle him.

Craig found his range with the forehand and soon picked up his first game. Another followed from his opponent's service, and the deficit was back to 3-2. The other player took a deep breath and sought out his coach, who responded with some hand signals.

Whatever they were seemed to work, and Craig lost the next two games, meaning he was serving to staying in the match. He powered down a brilliant ace, which drew a scream of delight from his sister, and his opponent returned the next two services into the net.

He won the next point too, leaving the score at 5-3. His team-mates all gathered around to watch, and although he battled hard and won a couple of points, in the end he went down 6-3.

'That's a much more respectable score,' grinned his coach. 'I think we've seen there's a lot more to your game than your results suggest. I'm delighted for you.'

Craig was still grinning when he bounced up the steps to where his mum and sister were sitting.

'Well done, son,' smiled his mum. 'That was a great recovery. We were just talking to that gentleman there who had lots of interesting ideas about how you could improve. Here he comes now.'

Craig turned to see the man in the turquoise tracksuit coming up the steps behind him two at a time.

The man stuck out his hand. 'Craig, isn't it. I'm Ingo. You, me, and your mum – we need to talk.'

CHAPTER 4

Joe hugged himself to keep warm, and hopped from one foot to the other. A cold wind was whipping along the quayside, and he could see waves starting to foam not far out in the bay. He expected it would be a rocky ride.

He looked around at his fellow travellers who were all keeping to themselves. They had arrived separately over the previous fifteen minutes, each ferried by taxi with just one suitcase and one sports bag for company.

They had been greeted by an elderly man who checked that they had come for the dawn ferry, and ticked their names off on a list. Joe sneaked a look at the list and saw there were just five names on it, which meant there was still one person to come.

He sidled up to the girl who was wearing the most sensible overcoat – a huge padded jacket with fur-lined hood.

'You came well-prepared,' he grinned. The girl smiled back. 'Yes, well they did mention we were going to an island, so I reckoned I'd stay dry. I'm Kim, by the way.'

Joe introduced himself and they compared the journeys they each had to take. Joe had been collected from his home just after midnight and had tried to sleep as the taxi sped across the country. Kim had travelled from a city just two hours away, and so had slept before her transport arrived. She was wide awake and buzzing about the journey ahead.

'It's all so mysterious,' she said. 'The taxi driver said I had to leave my mobile phone behind and wouldn't even tell me where we were going. He blacked out the windows towards the end of the journey so I couldn't see any road signs. Do you have any idea where we are?'

Joe shrugged his shoulders.

'I haven't a clue,' he admitted. 'I really wanted my phone to check the journey but I presume they'll let us know.'

But the old gentleman wouldn't answer any of their questions, just pointing at the last name on the list and tapping his wristwatch impatiently.

Joe wandered over to the other two youngsters and muttered 'good morning'.

They nodded back, concentrating on keeping their scarves over their faces as the first drops of rain started to fall.

'I'm Ajit,' said the taller of the two, while the other smiled and just said, 'Jess'.

'I wonder which boat we'll be taking,' said Kim, pointing at the array of small craft that were tied up along the quay.

'I hope it's not one of those row boats,' grinned Joe. 'But there's at least six of us so I suppose it must be that red one with the windows.'

They looked along the quay to where a small boat was tied up. It had a viewing platform on the top deck and looked like it was used to ferry tourists in the summer months.

'Yes, yes, that's the little beauty we'll be using today,' called out the old man, who was getting more agitated as he checked his watch more frequently. 'It's getting close to the time by which we will have to leave,' he sighed. 'Which means one of your group may have to miss the trip.'

'Could they come later?' asked Kim.

The old man chuckled. 'Later? … Heh, heh. They'll be a long time waiting around here for the next ferry for this particular trip.'

He gazed back through the night at the long road that led down to the quay.

'I'll give him five more minutes but then we'll have to go. Everyone climb aboard this one – carefully now – and make yourselves comfortable down below.'

Kim led the way across the gangplank onto the boat, skipping her hand along the icy handrail, afraid to grip it in case she got her fingers stuck to the frozen metal. She stooped as she descended into the lower cabin and flicked the switch to light up the inside.

There were rows of seats across the middle, and benches around the side, so she plonked herself down in the front and dumped her bags on the floor.

'Grab yourselves a life jacket,' the old man called down the stairway. 'They're in the red box at the bottom of the stairs.'

Joe, Jess, Ajit and Kim collected their life jackets and worked out how to put them on. Boarding the ship seemed to have changed their mood – they were slightly less con-cerned with the cold, but even more fearful and nervous about what lay ahead of them in what was left of the night.

They wandered around the lower deck, but with nothing but black night around them they ran out of things to see in seconds. Joe took a couple of steps up the staircase and poked his head back out above deck.

'All good down below?' enquired the old man, who was

starting to untie the cables that kept the boat moored to the quay.

'Yes, we're settled,' replied Joe. 'When will we be leaving?'

'Just as soon as I get us up and ready… three or four minutes I suppose.' He took one last look back over his shoulder and put his hand up to stop Joe speaking.

'Hold on, do you hear that?' He pointed into the night, where Joe could see nothing but blackness and hear nothing but the lapping of water.

'That's an engine… a Ford I reckon,' the old man started. 'Why has he got his lights off?'

Joe waited silently, and after a minute or so he could hear, faintly, the sound of a car accelerating. He watched where the old man said was the roadway, but it wasn't until the sounds of the engine were quite loud that the car's headlights were switched on. Joe could see it was moving very quickly, and the old man looked concerned.

'What's kept him… and what's the messing with the headlights?' he muttered as the car neared the quay. 'Here, youngster, give me a hand with this gangway. We may need to move off quickly.'

Joe came back on dry land and helped the old man with

his preparations as they waited for the final traveller to arrive. Although the man was stooped and wrinkled, he was remarkably agile and fast-moving for his age, and Joe got the impression he was stronger than he appeared too.

They were just ready to cast off when a black Ford taxi pulled up on the dock. The driver leapt out and went straight to the old man.

'I'm sorry we're late. We were followed, and I spent a lot of time shaking them off. I had to drive the last twenty kilometres with the lights off.' The old man nodded, and thanked him.

Joe helped the new arrival take his bags on board and showed him below. He raced back up to help the old man who was already hauling the gangplank on deck, a job Joe had reckoned would need two able-bodied men.

The taxi-man uncoupled the last rope and tossed it on board. Joe waved to him, and as he watched the driver return to his car, he noticed a pair of headlights appearing over the horizon. He pointed them out to the old man, who bit his lip.

'OK, we'll turn off all the cabin lights and get away from here as quickly as possible.'

He called out to the driver, and told him to go back a different way. 'Try to lead them astray, there'll be a good tip in it for you,' he shouted, getting a thumbs-up in return.

The old man took his place on the bridge, switching the engine into life and killing all the lights on board. 'Hold tight, it'll be a bumpy one,' he called out to the passengers.

Joe went down to join the others, who were looking increasingly nervous.

The new arrival smiled up at him, 'Thanks for the help with the bags, we were a bit frazzled there.'

'No worries. I'm Joe, by the way.'

'Cheers, my name's Craig.'

CHAPTER 5

The *Pirate Queen*, for that was the name of the craft, pulled away from the quay and out into the dark channel. Joe watched the old man as he guided the boat through the waves, nudging it from side to side as he took it through waters he appeared to know like the back of his hand.

They reached the end of the dockside where Joe spied a lighthouse flashing a warning, which spurred the old man to take a look back over his shoulder. There was no sign of any activity on the dock, and no sign of either of the cars. The taxi-man must have led the other driver away successfully, although why anyone would be chasing them and need such action was a complete mystery to Joe.

So much about the night was a complete mystery to him. His life had changed after the Woodstock game, and the meeting with Fry and his exotic hat, but he still didn't know why.

Joe remembered the horrible feeling in his stomach as he waited in the car while his parents had talked to the mysterious stranger who was pointing out things to them on an iPad. He just couldn't imagine what Fry wanted with his parents, and it wasn't helped that on their return they told him that they had been sworn to secrecy.

As they sat in the car his dad explained that Fry was there to tell him he had been selected for a unique educational and sporting opportunity that involved living away from home, but if they told Joe any more he would lose it. They told Joe they needed to think more about it, but said they had been reassured by Fry and their initial feelings were excitement for the chance it would give him.

Joe looked out the window as his friends' parents drove them away one by one and he wondered would he ever see them again. Joe trusted his parents knew best for him so when they told him he should go he accepted it, but he was still bursting with questions and, if he was honest, a little fearful. He looked at his mum who hadn't said much and he could tell she was on the verge of tears.

Joe spent the next two days in something of a daze, excited but nervous about what could possibly in store. He steered clear of his team-mates over the weekend, as much out of embarrassment that he didn't really know what was happening.

Two nights later his dad woke him up, told him to get dressed and ushered him downstairs where his mother had already packed his bags. Dad told him Fry had texted to say the taxi-man would be there at midnight.

They sat around and chatted awkwardly until he arrived, skirting the whole subject of why Joe was leaving while hoping he would be happy. They also told him they were very proud of him, although he couldn't work out why.

Joe had been ordered to either leave his mobile phone at home or hand it over to the driver for safe keeping, which he decided was the best option and at least offered some hope that he would get it back after some interval. His mum was most worried about this part, and asked Joe to promise he would let them know as soon as could that everything was all right.

The driver was friendly, but suggested that Joe get some sleep as it was a long drive and they wouldn't arrive till before first light. Joe had taken his advice and slept almost all the way, just waking briefly when the taxi-man stopped for petrol and slammed the boot. It was still dark as Joe scanned the east for the early signs of dawn breaking as the *Pirate Queen* ploughed through the bay, heading straight out to sea.

Joe looked around at the other four passengers. Kim seemed very nice, but reserved, and she looked the most relaxed about the journey. Ajit was bubbling with excitement – or nerves – and was unable to sit still as he raced from one side of the boat the other. Jess was also bouncing around, asking lots of questions despite no one being able to answer them. Craig looked very tired, perhaps the end of his journey had taken a lot out of him, and he didn't seem very interested in joining in conversations with the others.

Every few hundred metres a dark shape would loom out of the night as they passed another rocky crag or small island.

'There's a house on that one,' said Ajit, as a bulb flickered on in one of the homes in the distance. Further away still some lights were switched on as early-risers on the mainland awoke to start their day.

'Dawn coming soon,' called out the old man from the wheel-house. 'We haven't much time.'

The five children looked at each other.

'I really wish we knew what was going on,' said Kim.

'I suppose so, but it sounds as if it will be all clear soon enough, as long as he doesn't crash into an iceberg,' grinned Craig.

The rest laughed and studied the waves outside for any change in the seascape.

Joe pointed back to where they had come, where a faint golden glow had just crept above the horizon and the sound of seagulls screeching became more frequent.

'It won't be long until the sun's up. If he's racing the dawn he'd want to get a move on.'

CHAPTER 6

N one of the passengers were regular sea-goers, but they all agreed that the *Pirate Queen* seemed to speed up as soon as Joe made his suggestion.

'There's some seals!' squealed Jess as they passed a tiny, thin island on which perched dozens of the creatures. The rest of them marvelled at the creatures, but Joe and Kim tumbled as the boat took a sudden lurch to one side.

'Sorry about that,' called the old man. 'Had to take a quick short-cut, but we're nearly there.'

The five gathered at the front of the lower deck, scanning the sea ahead as the skies began to brighten.

'We seem to have left all the islands behind,' frowned Ajit. 'We're heading straight out into the ocean.'

The boat raced along for another three minutes before the old man called down to them again. 'Right, crew, hold tight as I'm going to swing her around again. We've arrived.'

Joe gripped the handrail and looked out at the waves – there was nothing to be seen as far as his eyes could focus.

Was the old man mad? What had he led them into?

After the *Pirate Queen* juddered to a halt, the old man switched off the engine and came downstairs.

'I hope you enjoyed your voyage on the old *Queen*,' he grinned, receiving a mixture of nods and shaken heads in return. 'Well, I can now tell you that we have arrived at our destination, and not a minute too soon. I'll just have time to tell you a little bit about our location. The town we left from is Westport, on the west coast. We are now out on the edge of Clew Bay, right where it meets the Atlantic Ocean.

'I don't expect many of you will heard of Clew Bay, but it is an ancient place full of legends and magical tales. We have had holy men and wicked women here, saints and pirates, and more islands than some of you can count.

'The wise old people know, however, that there are exactly three-hundred and sixty-five islands in the Bay, one for every day of the year. But the wisest of those people also know that once every four years, on the twenty-ninth day of February, another island makes a fleeting appearance. It doesn't stay around for long, maybe an hour, but Leap Island is the most magical place of all.'

The passengers stared open-mouthed at the old man as

he recounted the tale.

'Look,' gasped Joe, as he pointed to a strange rippling and bubbling in the water, just metres from their boat.

'Hold on,' snapped the old man, 'that swell will cause a big wave.'

The passengers held tight once more and watched in amazement as a huge bubble of water grew in the ocean, water rushing away from it as it rose into the air.

The bubble popped, revealing a small island about the size of two football fields laid end to end, with a steep rise at the western end to what appeared to be cliffs. Right in the middle, just before the terrain rose, stood a stone cottage with a rusting tin roof.

'Is that where we're going?' whispered Joe to Jess. 'Doesn't look much of an educational opportunity to me.'

When the waters had settled, the old man switched the engine back to life and sailed the *Pirate Queen* in as close as he could get to the new island. 'Right, we'll have to make the last few metres in the dinghy,' he announced.

He lowered a bright orange dinghy into the sea beside the boat and supervised the passengers as they loaded their luggage aboard first. He raced across to the island in less

than a minute and swiftly unloaded the bags before returning to the Pirate Queen.

'Be careful getting in and out of this,' he announced, 'you
don't want to end up in the Atlantic at this time of the year.'

The five children took his advice keenly, warily regarding
the black depths as they skipped across the ocean to the
shore. The old man helped them on to dry land, where they
rejoined their luggage as he pulled the dinghy on to the
grass.

'Well, here we are,' he grinned. 'You're all very welcome
to Leap Island.'

CHAPTER 7

Not much to it, though, is there?' sighed Kim, as she pointed from one end of the island to the other.

'Well ... There's more to Leap Island than meets the eye,' grinned the old man. 'And less to it, too,' he added playfully.

'Can you please tell us what we are doing here, sir?' asked Jess, who was looking extremely fed up.

'Well, first I'm just going to rest and relax for a while – it was a long night and in case you hadn't noticed I've been doing most of the work over the past hour.'

The old man sat down on a rock and took in his surroundings. 'I haven't been here in Clew Bay for four long years and I've been looking forward to enjoying the view,' he chuckled.

Joe and Ajit left down their bags and wandered off towards the cottage. Joe had a sinking feeling in his stomach – was this all a terrible hoax? Had his parents been conned into believing this was an amazing school – and he grew fearful at what exactly they had got themselves into.

'Don't go in there yet,' warned the old man. 'I have the key, anyway.'

Joe lifted his arm in acknowledgement and veered off towards the cliffs. They fell away sharply into the ocean, giving Leap Island the shape of a giant, thin slice of cake floating on the surface of the waves.

'Just think,' said Ajit, pointing out to sea. 'If we kept sailing in the *Pirate Queen* the next thing we'd hit would be America.'

'I think we'd hit the bottom of the petrol tank first, Ajit,' grinned Joe. 'That old rust-bucket wouldn't get us too far.'

'I hope this isn't some con that we've fallen for. My mum and dad told me it was an amazing place – but this looks like a dump.'

The pair turned back and strolled down the slope towards the cottage, whose white walls seemed even brighter than when they first spied it coming out of the waves. There were no windows anywhere in its walls, and the sole doorway was barred and secured with just a keyhole to suggest it could be guarding something inside.

'It sounds like we're going in there eventually,' said Joe. 'I could do with getting in out of this cold wind.'

They rejoined the others at the shore, where the old man was pointing out how far they had come as the other islands receded into the distance under the cold grey sky and the onshore headland was a faint black pimple far, far away.

'Did you see how steep those cliffs are, Joe?' asked the old man. 'It's like someone took an axe and chopped down on the island.'

Jess hugged herself and turned her back to the wind, which was starting to get stronger.

'Can you *please* tell us what we are doing here, or show us to someone who's in charge,' she asked the old man again, 'I really need to get in out of this gale before I freeze.'

The ferry pilot smiled back. 'Oh, all right then, let's get indoors and I can explain a little more.'

He led the five up the slope to the cottage before he stooped to open the lock. It took a couple of firm twists before it eventually opened.

'I suppose being used once every four years can't be good for a lock,' grinned the old man. 'Come through here now and watch your footing.'

The five peered nervously into the darkness and followed the old man as he walked through the doorway. He reached into the gloom and fumbled for the light switch before the room sprang to life.

The youngsters blinked as they took in their surprising new surroundings. The entire interior of the broken-down cottage was painted brilliant white, with shiny chrome handles inside the door and one-way windows looking out onto Leap Island.

'How do they do that?' asked Ajit, pointing at the windows.

'I think that's probably the least important question that springs to mind,' muttered Joe as he gazed around the room. He was most interested in the staircase that led down from the middle of the floor to a bright chrome doorway. The handle turned, and a tall man emerged, smiling up at them all before he ascended the steps.

'Ah, Kalvin,' said the old man, 'these are our latest recruits – Kim, Jess, Ajit, Craig and Joe. They seem a sprightly bunch, but now we need to warm them up a little.'

Kalvin nodded, clicked his fingers and the room was suddenly the temperature of hot buttered toast. 'Is that warm enough for you?' he asked.

Joe was glad that the bone-chilling cold was no more, but

still didn't feel too reassured at how easily Kalvin had done it. He exchanged a nervous glance with Kim.

'Welcome to Leap Island,' Kalvin said. 'I hope you all enjoy your stay here.'

'Yes, but can you please tell us what's going on?' asked Kim, again. 'This boatman doesn't seem to know what we are doing here, perhaps you can help us, or take us to some-one that does.'

'Gosh, no, I wouldn't be allowed to tell you such things, I have to go now to prepare the boat before he brings it back to mainland before the island submerges once more, which will happen in…' He checked his watch. 'Seven minutes and twenty-two seconds. So, I'd best be off.'

Kalvin made for the cottage door and turned back to address them. 'I suggest you head down the stairs as quickly as possible, and that "old boatman" will tell you what hap-pens next. After all, he's the reason you're all here – the other name for Leap Island is Atlantis. And this is its very own king, Victor the First.'

CHAPTER 8

You're the, eh ... King?' gasped Kim.

'I am indeed, Kim, but for now let us all make haste as my time is short,' replied Victor.

'Yes, my name is indeed Victor, although Kalvin is the only one allowed to call me "King". It's his little joke. He's been working for me for many years and is an important part of my team as you will come to learn. It was good to get to know you all a little during the long night we had getting here, but you won't be seeing much of me over the next few months. I am going to bid my farewell now, and shortly you will meet Luce who manages the Atlantis Academy for me. She will explain all.'

And with that Victor went back out through the door by which they had entered.

Kalvin returned and ushered the five down the steps and through a heavy steel door. Joe helped him push it back into place, and to swing the bolts into place to seal it.

He showed them through into another room, where there

were rows of airplane-style seats.

'Strap yourselves in,' he told them. 'It won't take long, but the first wave can throw you off your feet, so it is best to be careful.'

The five youngsters did as they were told while Kalvin checked the door once more before seating himself at the head of the row and clicking his belt.

He checked his watch and counted down. '8... 7... 6... 5.... Hold tight now... 3... 2... ...'

Joe felt the room take a huge lurch upwards, and everything within the walls rattled violently. He was glad he was strapped down, as he was sure he would be flying around like a rag doll if was not. Just as quickly, he had the sensation of the room falling quickly, before landing softly.

Kalvin unclicked his belt and stood.

'I never get used to that,' he grinned. 'Is everyone OK?'

The youngsters nodded, and each undid their seat belt.

'What do you think has happened?' asked Craig.

'Dunno, maybe there was an earthquake?' suggested Ajit.

Joe shook his head. 'It's weird, but the island just appeared out of the ocean. Kalvin said something about it submerging. Maybe it's just sunk back under water again?'

'So, we're under the sea in some giant green submarine?' gasped Jess, sounding increasingly panicked.

'Well…'

With that, another door swung open at the back of the room and in walked six people, each dressed in differently-coloured tracksuits.

'He was at my tennis match,' Craig whispered to Joe, pointing at the man with the turquoise outfit.

'And that's Kelly, I met her at rugby,' said Kim.

The six adults lined up at the top of the room, before a tall woman dressed in red took a step forward.

'Good morning, I know you've all had a long and arduous journey and you will be shown to your bedrooms as soon as I'm finished here. I do, however, have a few things to explain which will help you sleep easier, I hope,' she smiled.

'Leap Island is home to Atlantis Academy,' she started, 'And you five are our first new pupils in four years. Our island only emerges from the sea for one hour every four years and on each occasion we bring five new children on board.'

Joe looked along the line of adults, recognising the smallest one as the man with the stylish black hat. He was in a black tracksuit now and stared straight ahead.

'But what *is* Atlantis Academy?' asked Craig. 'I've never heard of it – what sort of school is it?'

'Well, you're right, it is a school,' replied Luce, 'but it is a lot more than that. We have assembled the greatest minds and teachers in the world to train the five of you to be the very best you can be.'

'And what's that?' asked Joe.

'Well, in your case, Joe, that is a footballer.'

Joe's face reddened, and he snorted. 'You've got to be joking,' he laughed. 'Even my coach says I have two left – or rather right – feet.'

The small man in the black tracksuit stepped forward.

'No, Joe, your coach was wrong. Very wrong. You are eleven years old now – by the time you are finished in Atlantis Sports Academy you will be fifteen. And you will be the very best fifteen-year-old footballer in the world.'

CHAPTER 9

Junior Wimbledon? They have *got* to be joking,' said Craig, as he lifted his suitcase onto his bed.

'And they think I could be playing minor hurling for the county AND international cricket too,' laughed Ajit.

Craig, Ajit and Joe were now room-mates, and were settling into their new home.

'This is class,' said Joe, exploring the large room that contained three beds, storage areas and desks, on each of which sat a shiny new computer, each a different colour. He pushed the 'on' button, but nothing happened.

'They said they'd install all that stuff later, once we had some sleep,' grinned Ajit.

'How do they expect us to sleep,' asked Joe. 'I know we've been up all night but my head is buzzing at what they told us – and all this,' he added, with the sweep of an arm.

'So, are you some sort of star footballer?' Craig asked him.

'Not at all,' laughed Joe. 'I'm the opposite. I'm easily the worst player on my team, and we're close to the worst team in our league. For them to say that is just taking the mickey.'

After they got dressed for bed, Joe explained the sequence of events that led him to this strange location, and after he had finished Craig told his story too.

Ajit expelled a deep breath and grinned at the pair of them. 'I suppose I'd better explain why I'm here too – but you'll have to promise not to laugh.'

'My mum and dad came here from India about twenty years ago, and my little sisters and I were all born here. Dad loves cricket, but there were no teams near where we live so he just follows it on the internet and TV now.

'About two or three years ago he bought me a bat and started to teach me about the game. It was just the two of us in the local park, and sometimes mum and my sisters would help running for the ball. I love it, especially batting, and really enjoyed hitting the ball as far as I could.

'We started playing hurling in school and I liked that too, but I'm not very good at it. It was harder to concentrate too, as in cricket you have to focus on every ball, but in hurling my mind drifted when the ball was up the other end. You hold the bat and the hurl in different ways, too, so I kept getting mixed up.

'Then last week we had a game against a city team. My mind was wandering and I was actually playing a few cricket shots in the air when one of my team-mates called out my name. I was in another world but just caught sight of the sliotar – the ball – coming towards me.

'I just stepped out to it like I was playing a drive in cricket and connected with it absolutely perfectly. The ball just took off and was still rising when it went between the posts for a point.'

Joe laughed. 'That must have been a shock to them.'

'It certainly was?' said Ajit. 'The lads were delighted, but the old guy who coaches us was a bit grumpy about it afterwards, even though it was the only point we scored in the whole second half.

'Oh yeah, I forgot to mention that I play on the half-back line. When I hit the point I was about ten metres inside our own half. The ball went about sixty metres before it crossed the bar, and probably would have gone another thirty or more. The ref nearly swallowed his whistle.'

'Wow,' gasped Craig. 'And was there someone watching from the Academy?'

'There was,' shrugged Ajit. 'I can't imagine she was there

just to watch me, but she came up to my parents after the game and said she wanted to talk to them. They never told me what was in store – but … well, here I am.'

CHAPTER 10

In their room, Kim and Jess were also getting used to their new surroundings.

'I keep pinching myself,' Jess announced as she finally lay down on her bed. 'This whole night has been so hard to take in. It still feels like a weird dream.'

'Yeah, it's like when you've had a piece of cheese at bedtime,' replied Kim. 'At least that's what my mam always warns me about.'

'I'm trying not to think too much about being deep under the water, and what happens if there's a leak,' said Jess. 'You don't think there could be one, do you?'

'No!' chuckled Kim. 'I'm sure they keep a close watch on that sort of thing. I wouldn't mind if we had a window, or a porthole I think it's called. It would be so cool to watch the fish swimming past.'

Jess laughed. 'So, you're going to be a rugby star, according to that woman with the clipboard. What do you make of that?'

'Well, I don't really get it to be honest,' said Kim, after she explained how she had come to be among the new intake at the Academy. 'I'm not that good, but I really enjoy it and would love to get better. Maybe that's why they picked me out. Kelly – that's the lady with the clipboard – seems really nice though. What's your story, anyway?'

Jess stretched her arms out wide and yawned. 'Oh, I'm nothing special either. I like running, and the man from this place came to see our school sports day.

'I'm not joking when I say I'm in the bottom half in my year in every event. I didn't win any races, or even win a medal, but I suppose he was impressed that I entered everything from 100 metres up to the 800 metres. I even ran in the hurdles and did the long jump. He told me I'm going to be in the Olympics – which is just silly.'

'I know, it does all seem a bit far-fetched, and for the boys too,' replied Kim. 'They seem to be fairly average at their games.

'But there must be something they see in us – I can't understand why they would have organised all this and spent all the money they must have for a giant practical joke that almost no-one will see. It just doesn't make sense.

AND I really miss my mobile phone!'

Jess yawned again. 'Well, I'm not going to let it worry me or ruin my sleep. We'll have time enough for working out what's going on after some rest.' And with that she rolled over, switched off her bedside light, and fell fast asleep.

Kim smiled. She liked Jess, and the three boys seemed nice too. Atlantis Academy sounded like it would be a bit of a challenge, but a lot of fun too. She brushed her teeth and noticed her favourite brand of toothpaste was provided, as were other items around the bathroom. Luce and her team had obviously done their homework on her, and the others.

But before she let another wave of questions sweep through her brain she told herself that going to sleep was now the most important thing she needed to do, so she did.

CHAPTER 11

The youngsters were awoken four hours later by the ringing of an alarm, followed by Luce's voice coming over a loudspeaker.

'I'm sorry to disturb you but it is important that you all get up now. It is vital that you get your sleep back to a normal pattern and last night's activity has thrown you all out of line. If you get up now and then return to bed after six hours, you should be back in your usual groove tomorrow.

'So, please get up and dressed – wear the packet of clothes labelled "day one" which is in your personal wardrobe. When you are ready open your door and you will be brought to the canteen for lunch.'

'Lunch! Now that's good news,' yelped Craig as he leapt out of bed, stood up and stretched. Joe and Ajit were less enthusiastic about leaving what were very comfortable beds indeed.

Shaking the sleep out of his head, Joe wandered into the bathroom to wash his face. As he stood in front of the mirror a drawer slid open beneath it which contained soap – in a black wrapper – as well as shampoo and a face cloth, all with his name on them. He gently touched the 'hot' button and lovely warm water flowed out of the tap. Craig was already in the shower, singing a song about how he did like to be beside the seaside.

In their own very different ways the trio got themselves ready, finally ripping open the plastic packet that surrounded their new clothing.

'Yuck,' gasped Craig, as he lifted out a tracksuit in bright turquoise and a pair of matching runners.

Joe grinned, a lot happier that the kit he had been allocated was jet black, while Ajit was a bit less sure about the yellow tracksuit he was expected to wear.

'We look like something off toddlers' television,' complained Craig as they opened the door to the corridor outside, where Kim and Jess were waiting in their outfits of red and green, respectively.

'Well, you two got some sensible colours anyway,' grinned Joe, as he gestured back at his room-mates. 'I hope they change the colours every day. I could get a headache looking at Craig.'

'I don't know, Joe,' smiled Jess. 'I think black makes you look like one of the baddies in one of those space adventure films. I hope you're not a baddie?'

Joe was still laughing when Luce arrived.

'Well, I'm glad to see you're enjoying yourselves. I suppose one thing about the unorthodox way you got here is that you've all started to make friends, which is a good thing. Atlantis Academy should be a lot of fun, but it's always better to have a few pals to lean on if things get difficult – and there will downs as well as ups. Now, follow me and we'll see how well your appetite has survived that long voyage.'

Craig was first to the buffet, where Angela, who worked in the kitchen, welcomed him and handed him a turquoise plate to match his tracksuit. He took a step back as his eyes focused on the food on display.

'Eh, I think we'll need someone to translate this food into English, please,' he said. 'Is it edible? And where are the chips?'

Luce smiled and stepped in front of the cabinet where the food was displayed.

'Now, Craig, don't tell me you haven't seen any of these foods before?' she grinned, as she pointed at a range of cold meats, salads and wraps. 'We're not going to be totally down on your favourite foods, but it *is* a sports academy and we want you to be full of the ideal fuels to drive the important machine that is your body. There will be a time and a place for burgers, even sausages, but I think after your classes on nutrition you will probably never want to eat such things again.'

Craig snorted. 'You've got to be joking. I *love* a good fry for breakfast at the weekend….'

'Well, we'll see what we can do about that,' chuckled Luce. 'For now, tuck in to the turkey and try some of those little nutty things. They're very tasty if you dip them in that,' she added pointing at a beige substance in a little pot.

Craig selected the food Luce had suggested. 'Better still, stick it all in a wrap with some lettuce, beetroot and tomato,' she added.

'Uh, you lost me at "lettuce",' replied Craig, 'but I'll give the rest of it a go.'

He piled the food onto his plate; instead of a cash register at the end of the line Angela was waiting to run the plate into a scanner that recorded what each student was choosing to eat.

The other four lined up at the buffet and also found plenty to eat, and they all joined Craig and Luce at the table.

'This is really good,' mumbled Craig as he chewed on his lunch.

'Excellent,' said Luce, 'It's good to see you're open to a few changes. Now, relax for a while, enjoy your meal and we'll head into the classroom and I'll fill you in on what this is all about.'

Luce left the five of them to eat and chat. Craig demolished his wrap and went back for a second helping.

'That brown stuff is very tasty,' he told the other four.

'Oh yeah, that's hummus,' said Kim. 'They make it out of chick peas, oil and sesame seeds.'

Craig's face fell. 'Chick peas? Yuck!'

'But you loved it a minute ago,' laughed Ajit.

'Well that was before I knew what was in it,' snapped Craig.

'Oh well, maybe this next class will let you know what they put inside sausages,' grinned Jess.

CHAPTER 12

Luce wasn't in a jokey mood anymore when they assembled in the classroom. She even looked slightly worried, Joe thought.

'Right, as we said earlier, you are all here because our team of coaches and scouts have spent months seeking out the five boys and girls who we believe we can turn into the very best in their chosen sport over the next four years. None of you were the best in the country, in fact most of you were among the worst in your club or school team.

'But we see in you a passion for the game, a willingness to work, and several other qualities that we consider more important than raw talent.

'You are here because we have promised your parents that besides being transformed into sporting superheroes, you will also receive the finest education imaginable. Each of you should be capable of being accepted for university by the age of fifteen, no matter your current level of educational attainment.

'We have reassured your parents that you will be looked after in every way, so if any of you have any concerns or problems please come and discuss them with me at any time. Our years on this island have shown us that happy kids are hard-working kids and we too will work hard to make sure you are happy.

'Atlantis Academy will provide you with everything you require for those four years, but you must commit to working hard and following to the letter the instructions you are given. This is not a prison, and we will listen to your point of view in every instance, but when we make a decision you must follow it.

'There will be one week's holidays a year, when you will be reunited with your family in a secret location. You will not be able to return to your home for four years however.'

Kim gasped. 'Really? But my friends … my puppy … four years …'

Luce ignored Kim's plea.

'You will be permitted thirty minutes every month to communicate via a secure video phone line, and you can see your pets then as well as your families. But talking of communications brings me to the first serious problem we have come across.'

Luce stared down at the five pupils.

'We understand that you were not brought into the initial decision to come here, but now that you are aboard we have a few unbreakable rules that we expect you to follow. The first should have been stressed to you by your taxi driver, and it concerns the use of telephones, tablets, laptops or any devices that can communicate with the world outside Atlantis Academy.'

Joe nodded and cast a sideways glance at his classmates. They were all unhappy to have given up their mobiles and would take some time to get used to it. He had got his phone for his eleventh birthday and knew he was already addicted to its bright lights and easy action.

Luce continued.

'You remember the man who brought you here on the ferry? Well Victor is a very, very rich man. Imagine that you had won a million euro on the lottery every single day since you were born – you still wouldn't be as wealthy as Victor. But he is a very good man, and very generous to people less well off than he is.

'However, he does have rivals and enemies, and he is

almost never seen in public for reasons of his personal safety. He is scrupulous about security and goes to great lengths to ensure he cannot be tracked nor Atlantis Academy discovered by those who may wish to harm it or steal its wonderful secrets.

'Which brings me to the fact that one of you has broken that unbreakable rule. One of you has a mobile phone hidden in your room. Please step forward.'

Joe's mouth opened in surprise. He looked down the line of his classmates and saw Craig staring at the floor before looking up and taking a step towards Luce. His face was bright red, but he also looked terrified.

'Thank you, Craig, for your honesty, and instant admission. Had you not done so you would be making a lonely journey home tonight. However, we have decided to give you one more chance, a luxury that will not be applied to anyone else. Your phone will be confiscated and returned at the end of your time here.

'The reason we were so concerned is because we believe Craig's phone has been tracked. His taxi was followed all the way to the quayside in Westport, and we detected some suspicious activity around the waters of Clew Bay this morning. They never came near enough to detect us, but it has forced us to change our plans and to plot a different course to our first destination.

'But that isn't anything for you to worry about as we won't arrive there for several weeks. A submarine island doesn't travel nearly as fast as an ocean liner you know,' she added, with a smile.

'What are we going to do till we get there?' asked Kim.

'Do?' replied Luce. 'Why, this is where the work will be done to prepare you. We have classrooms, laboratories, gyms, an indoor sports hall, sporting simulators… all under the sea. Come, it's now time for the guided tour.'

She led the five out of the room down a corridor lined with portraits of sportswomen and sportsmen.

'That's your man, the guy that won the Masters!' gasped Ajit.

'Yes,' smiled Luce. 'He was such a nice boy, but couldn't drive the ball twenty metres when he first came here.'

'And she won the 100-metres at the last Worlds,' squealed Jess, pointing at the second photo.

'At the start she couldn't break into a jog without tripping over her feet,' grinned Luce. 'She's really nice too – I asked her to telephone your parents to reassure them about the Academy. I think it was her call that convinced them to let you come!"

Jess's eyes widened. 'Wow – *she* rang my mum and dad?'

'Did *all* these people go to Atlantis Academy,' asked Joe, scanning the faces along the wall and recognising many as sporting superstars.

'Of course, that's why they are hanging here. This is our hall of fame. We have five empty spaces down here, ready for you.'

CHAPTER 13

L uce led the five into the first room; it was carpeted with artificial grass, but the youngsters were otherwise underwhelmed. All there was to see was one long blank white wall, and a cupboard at the back of the room.

'Not much going on here,' muttered Ajit. The others sniggered.

'Do you think so?' smiled Luce. 'Perhaps, but let's see what's on the menu this evening.'

The manager opened the cupboard, which was full of shelves packed with sporting equipment. There was also a control panel, which she flicked into life.

'Right now, you're the rugby player, aren't you?' she asked Kim, who nodded.

She tossed Kim a rugby ball and a kicking tee and flicked another switch. Up on the screen came a set of goal posts.

'So, without having to go outdoors in the cold and the wind of the winters back home, you can practise your kicking skills here.'

Kim set up the ball and duly planted it between the posts.

'Now try it from out on the touchline,' suggested Luce, adjusting the picture so Kim was now kicking from a tighter angle.

Again, the student smashed the ball over the bar.

'Hmmm, impressive,' smiled Luce. 'Now let's get a taste of that winter I talked about…'

She flicked another switch, and suddenly the temperature dropped, and a howling gale blew across the room.

Kim blew on her hands and leaned into the wind, but despite a strong kick the ball was caught by the wind and carried wide.

'Good effort, Kim. Now you can see just a few of the tricks we can come up with to help you practise for every situation. And not just for rugby.'

She flicked more buttons, and up flashed a football goal complete with a virtual image of a goalkeeper.

'The computer is in control of the keeper and competes against you to try to save the ball.'

Joe's eyes widened.

'Now, Craig, you collect the tennis racket from the shelf there and let's see how you get on against our friend Roger.'

Craig's jaw dropped as the screen changed to show a tennis legend standing there grinning back at him, all dressed in white.

'Would you prefer to play him on grass, clay or hard court?' asked Luce.

Craig shrugged. 'Hard, I suppose…'

The ground beneath the star switched colour and Luce tossed Craig a couple of tennis balls.

'Take your time,' grinned the onscreen Roger.

Craig gulped, and smashed the first serve into the virtual net. He paused, hopped the ball a couple of times, and served again.

The ball cleared the net, and his opponent returned it to Craig's backhand. The youngster was so surprised he fluffed the return, which he sliced into the net.

'Hard luck,' called Roger before fading into nothing when the picture disappeared.

'A bit of work to do, but you'll have the very best people to practise against,' grinned Luce. 'Don't worry, that wasn't him – he's programmed to occasionally speak some words to encourage you.'

The five were by now completely impressed by Luce and

her cupboard of tricks.

'There's a lot to take in here, and I'm going to introduce you to it sparingly, so perhaps we'll move straight to the laboratory where we have some paperwork to do. In fact, you'll probably spend the next two days in the labs as we amass as much data as we can about you.

'For example, our computers have worked out that most of the best tennis players – boys and girls – are 1.47 metres tall at the age of ten. We will work out, therefore, if you are unlikely to graduate as a tennis player and might be better switching sports to, say, golf.'

Craig went white.

'No, Craig, I'm not talking about you, that is just an example. We have ideal weight and height profiles for every age, and every sport. And every position on every sports team. We will also measure each of your major bones, your eyesight, even the length of your toes. We use the very latest medical and scientific knowledge to ensure you have the very best chance to be the very best in your sport.'

'If we're too small, or too big, do you make us bigger, or smaller?' asked Jess.

'No. We do not take radical approaches such as surgery,

or chemicals,' answered Luce. 'But there are other ways to make you grow taller which will be safe and honest.

'You will never, EVER, be offered anything to take which would provide a chemical short-cut to sporting success. Victor is passionately opposed to anything that gets in the way of clean sport and hates how some sportsmen and women have resorted to what they call "doping" for better results.'

'Yeah, doping is for dopes, that's what our coach always says,' chipped in Jess.

Everyone laughed.

'We want you all to be better people when you leave here – healthier, happier, cleverer, and if possible, more successful at your chosen sport. But that is the least important consideration, so you will not have to worry about being asked to take anything that would give you an edge illegally.

'But we will be measuring – and sometimes controlling – your intake of food and drinks, and you will be required to wear a device, like a wristwatch, which will measure your movements, your exercise, and your sleep.

'But most of all, we want this to be a time you look back on with pleasurable memories. So, once we're finished in the lab, I'll take you to Atlantis Island's own private cinema…'

CHAPTER 14

Joe tossed and turned in bed, annoyed with himself. He never had trouble sleeping, and especially after such a long, packed day he was surprised that his eyes refused to close. He knew it wasn't the fault of the eyes though, more that his brain was racing at two hundred kilometres per hour. He pinched himself once or twice, still struggling to believe that it all wasn't a crazy, vivid dream.

'OK,' he said to himself. 'So, some mad old billionaire decides to set up a sports school, sticks it underneath an island that doubles as a giant submarine, packs it with the latest technology, at enormous cost, to produce the greatest sportsmen and sportswomen in the world, and invites just five kids who are pretty rubbish at sport to become its pupils. One of whom is me.'

Joe was now overjoyed at the opportunity, delighted to be at a school where football was one of the subjects, and wasn't fazed at the huge amount of technology and new ideas with which they had been bombarded since they had arrived.

He wasn't even worried about missing his friends and family – they had moved around a lot when he was younger and his dad was working for the government, and he was happy that they would meet up for a holiday at some stage. And although he might not see his friends for four years, he thought Jess, Ajit, Kim and Craig were all really sound and he saw them as good pals already.

But still he could not sleep. It wasn't the soft hum of whatever giant engines were driving the island around the ocean – he had got used to that very quickly – and there was certainly no side-to-side sensation of being in any sort of ship. No, he knew it was all in his head, his excited brain refusing to lie still until it had seen everything the Academy had to offer.

He sat up in bed and twisted his legs over the side. The other boys were fast asleep, but he tried to be as silent as he could as he slipped his runners on, opened the door, and slid out into the corridor.

He took a quick look up and down, working out where he was as he was still getting his bearings on the island. He checked his watch – or rather the fitness device they had fitted on his wrist, which also told the time – and saw it was almost an hour past midnight.

He wasn't sure what he wanted to do, but reckoned he'd like to see more of the island without there always being a track-suited guide keeping an eye on him. He opted to turn left, heading back towards the way they had first come in. He came to the heavy, steel door that had closed behind them as the island sank into the waves and looked around. He decided to head down a passageway that was not as well-lit as the other, so he switched on the light on his wrist device.

It was colder here, and he held tight to the handrail that led him up a staircase to the next level, dozens of steps away. A low, greenish light meant he could find his way without tripping, but he needed the torch on his wrist to check his surroundings. He tried a couple of doors, which were locked, but as he neared a third it slid across automatically.

Joe peered inside, but all he could see in the tight space was three round windows. He took two steps across and wiped a film of water from the middle one, before bending to look through it.

He leapt back in shock, before stepping forward again.

Through the window all he could see was the ocean, but not the fish-tank type of view he might have expected. He was far, far above the waves, looking down as they crashed against the exterior walls of the island – or what he now recognised as the steep cliffs he and Ajit had explored back in Clew Bay.

'This window must be built into the cliff,' he thought, 'but when did we get to the surface?'

He watched the waves as they thundered against the rock face and marvelled at how stable the island was in such a storm. He scanned the dark horizon, and thought he spotted some specks of light, presumably a far-off island.

A noise somewhere off in the distance inside Atlantis broke his concentration and reminded him that he ought to be getting back to bed. He retraced his steps back to the room, meeting no-one on the way, and slipped under the covers before falling into a rapid, and deep, sleep.

CHAPTER 15

The next day was bewildering for Joe, and the rest of the Atlantis Academicals. The morning was spent having every single bone, joint and muscle in his body tested and measured. Every tooth was probed, almost every inch of his frame scanned and x-rayed as the medical staff built a complete record of the students' physiques.

Then they were tested over a range of activities, such as how high or how long they could jump, with a run and from a standing start. They were timed walking and running over 10 metres, 20 metres and 30 metres, and timed running backwards too. They were asked to kick every type and shape of ball that was designed to be kicked, and to hit others with bats, rackets or clubs. Every moment of the tests was filmed from several angles.

At the end of the day, exhausted and irritable, the last thing they wanted was a lecture from Luce, but that was what they got. Wearing her red tracksuit, she too was in a bad mood.

'All right, I'll keep this short as I'm sure you're tired after an arduous day. What we learned today will be at the heart of everything you do in the Academy over the next four years. We have learned your strengths, perhaps some of your weaknesses, and the areas you need to work hardest on. There will be hard decisions to be made based on this information, and we may decide that you should switch sports to one where you have a better chance of success.

'But first, we will work on improving your movement and physical flexibility. Victor has long been convinced that the very best sport that all great players must master first is gymnastics. For that is the sport that forces you to know how your body works, and how it can be best equipped for whatever you want it to do.

'Think of any game and then think how gymnastics can help – a speedy half-back can bounce and shimmy their way past a defender, a tennis player who can leap higher can deliver a more powerful serve, as with a bowler in cricket. There are many ways in which this works.

'So tomorrow you will start an intensive course which will give you a basic knowledge of gymnastics. Your teacher is a former student of this academy – when she came here she was an aspiring hockey star, but became so consumed by gymnastics that she switched over. You may recognise her – she won a gold and bronze medal at the last Olympic Games.'

Craig shrugged his shoulders. 'Hmmm. I think I missed that event,' he chuckled.

'Now, now,' said Jess. 'Gym is cool, we did loads of it in school. It's great for putting you in a good mood and I'm sure you'd look great in turquoise tights, Craigie…'

The rest of the class laughed, and even Craig had to smile.

'And I think I know who Luce is talking about,' said Ajit. 'She was on the TV news the night she won. It was the first time anyone from our country won a gymnastics medal.'

Joe nodded too, remembering the excitement at the Olympic medal ceremony and the two days when everyone out playing on the street was a would-be gymnast. Lads borrowed their sisters' ballet tights and swung out of tree branches, others walked around on their hands. But then someone else won a medal at show jumping and the gang all ran around slapping their backsides and leaping over the neighbours' fences instead, and the glory of gymnastics was soon forgotten.

'I have one other thing I need to talk to you about,' announced Luce. 'I appreciate that you may get bored here and may need to satisfy your spirit of adventure.'

Joe instantly blushed and looked towards the floor. He could feel Luce's eyes burrowing through the top of his head.

'Last night, one of you went exploring in the outer areas of the Academy. While there are very few areas of our home that remain off limits – and nobody breached them last night – I must caution you to be careful wandering around in the darkness.'

As Joe had his head down, the other four all looked at one another for clues. They weren't long realising who had been the midnight wanderer.

'Was it you, Joe?' asked Kim.

Joe nodded. 'I couldn't sleep and went for a walk. I didn't touch anything, honestly.'

Luce smiled. 'I know – we monitor your sleep and activity twenty-four hours a day, and we knew exactly what you were up to. We tracked you all the way up to the viewing room, and all the way back to bed. But I don't blame you. You all must still have lots of questions, and I will arrange for you to take another tour of the island that will show you how it works. And I will also explain to you something that Joe discovered last night.'

The four all looked again at Joe, who shrugged his shoulders.

CHAPTER 16

What Joe found out last night was that the island is moving south, and at top speed,' started Luce, looking down at the faces which showed expressions ranging from confusion to concern.

She tapped on the whiteboard behind her, which lit up to show a map of the Atlantic Ocean.

'You will all recall that we submerged shortly after you came aboard in Clew Bay. And that I mentioned that we noticed some strange activity there and had changed course. Well, we have decided to put some distance between us and whatever caused that, and so we have been steaming along under the Atlantic for the last two days,' she said, trailing her index finger along the map showing the route they had travelled.

'To save fuel, the captain decided last night to surface, which is why you were able to see the waves and the sky through the portholes, Joe,' she explained. 'It was a clear night and there was no shipping within eighty kilometres of us, or land within five hundred kilometres, so it was a good opportunity to rest the craft.

'We are currently heading for the Caribbean where we will be able to surface and take our place, disguised as part of a tiny, uninhabited archipelago. We will stay there for a few weeks to allow maintenance for the island and rest for the crew – although you five will still be working and doing most of your activities inside here. We will, however, allow you out for some sunshine time,' she smiled.

The five all began talking at once, excited at the prospect of a beach holiday in the West Indies, no matter how little time they would be allowed to enjoy it.

'You will learn more as we reach our destination in two or three days, but in the meantime I want you to get plenty of sleep'– she stared at Joe – 'and throw yourselves whole-heartedly into the gymnastics tomorrow. I will organise a full tour of the moving parts of Atlantis too.'

And with that, Luce was gone, leaving the students to pile into Joe with questions about his midnight tour.

'Where did you go, Joe?'

'What did you see?'

'Is it dangerous?'

Joe explained his short excursion to his classmates, telling them about the cliff-face room from where he watched the Atlantic storm.

'It was terrifying,' he admitted. 'I was further up with Ajit when we went there the first day, but it was sort-of calm then. This was a raging storm and the waves were smashing into the island. I don't know how it remains so steady – I nearly got seasick looking at it.'

'I hope they bring us up there to see the cliffs too,' said Jess. 'I'd love to try out my new binoculars.'

That reminded Joe. 'Yeah, it's hard to work out the horizon – especially at night – but I did see a couple of red lights from a ship, or an island.'

'Really?' asked Kim. 'Luce said we were hundreds of kilometres from anywhere …'

Joe shrugged. 'I don't know, I definitely saw lights flashing.'

'Maybe it was a plane – or those guys from the taxi following us,' said Craig.

'Maybe you should let Luce know,' suggested Ajit.

'Yeah… maybe I should,' replied Joe. 'It was probably the Northern Lights or something …'

'Off the coast of Florida?' laughed Jess.

Joe chuckled too before setting off to find Luce.

CHAPTER 17

Luce was concerned after Joe had told her what he had seen.

'You should have mentioned this before now,' she snapped.

'I'm sorry,' Joe replied, 'It was only when Kim reminded me that you said we were miles from anything that I thought it might be suspicious.'

She motioned him to follow her. 'We will see what our security officer thinks about this.'

Luce led Joe down another spiral staircase to a brightly lit corridor with offices on either side behind glass walls. At the very end was a red door which Luce tapped on twice.

'Come in,' came the reply, and Luce entered, followed by Joe.

'Ah, this is Joe,' said the security officer, a tall man with a bushy moustache. 'My name is Ross. I was checking out your night-time rambles earlier. You certainly seem an adventurous chap.'

Joe smiled thinly.

'We're here because Joe thinks he saw something outside last night,' started Luce.

Ross frowned. 'We had surfaced by then, hadn't we,' he mused. 'There was nothing within range that you would have been able to see.'

'Well, I definitely saw something,' insisted Joe. 'I was in the room at the top of the cliffs and saw lights flashing. It was hard to tell, but they seemed like they were a good few kilometres away.'

Ross drew a circle on his writing pad and asked Joe to show exactly where the lights were in the sky as he looked out the porthole. Joe thought for a few seconds and described them to Ross as he plotted them on the paper – one big light that flickered on and off away on the horizon, with two smaller lights that stayed on for as long as he was looking at them.

'OK, thank you for that, Joe, now please return to your quarters while I have a chat with Luce.'

Joe let himself out and wandered back along the glass corridor. He peered through into the offices, which were full of desks – maybe twenty in all – but at which only two people sat. There was a huge map of the world on one wall, with a blinking light in the middle of the Atlantic Ocean which

Joe presumed was some sort of 'You Are Here' symbol.

He found his way back to the living quarters where Ajit and Craig were having a heated argument about who got to use the shower first.

'I put my yellow towel on the handle and said I "bagsied" it first,' said Ajit.

'You snooze, you lose,' laughed Craig. 'I didn't see any towel.'

'Come on, you've sneaked in first every day so far,' complained Ajit.

'Every day? We've only been here two days!' laughed Craig. 'If you want to get it first then get here first.'

Joe stepped between them. 'Hang on, hang on,' he pleaded. 'Let's work this out. We've one shower, and three sweaty future legends. How about we take it in turns to go first. Yesterday was Craig, today it's Ajit, and I don't mind waiting till tomorrow to go first. You fire away Ajit, and Craig can be second, but tomorrow he's third.'

The two other boys stared at Joe, trying to work out in their heads what he had suggested.

'Eh…. OK,' said Ajit, slipping past Craig into the

shower cubicle.

Craig shrugged and went back to his bed and picked up a magazine.

'Four years is an awful long time Craig,' said Joe. 'No point picking rows over stupid things this early. We're going to have to get to like and trust each other.'

CHAPTER 18

Luce and Ross spent the next hour going back over video recordings of the island's voyage over the previous day. There were sensors, cameras, radar and other ways of keeping tabs on the journey and anything the island came into contact with. There were no cameras recording from the precise position that Joe had been standing, but higher up on the cliff was a high-definition recorder which scanned the horizon.

'We can narrow it down to the precise two minutes Joe was in the room, and he seems to have been looking towards north-north-east that he saw these lights...' said Ross.

He twiddled with the computer and zoomed the screen to show the narrow area Joe would have seen at that precise time.

'Radar and sonar are clear, so there were no planes or submarines in the area....' Ross muttered.

'What's that?' asked Luce, pointing to the corner of the screen.

'It looks like a shooting star, but it's moving too slowly,' he replied.

He zoomed in even closer, showing three red lights flickering in the sky in a fixed position. Just as Joe had said, one looked slightly bigger than the other.

'Can you get a fix on it?' asked Luce.

'I'll try,' replied Ross, 'I'll try to blow the picture up a little more.'

He flicked a couple of keys on the keyboard and the screen filled with what appeared to be a giant flying insect.

'Yuk,' said Luce, 'that's an evil-looking creature.'

'That's no creature,' said Ross. 'It's a drone. And from the looks of it, it's following us.'

They spent the next couple of hours having the first of their classes in academic subjects. Their maths teacher was a tiny, bald man who was very enthusiastic about the subject and his eyes sparkled as he told them about his favourite numbers. It was like no other maths class any of them had every had and they were wide-eyed as he explained about numbers and their different uses and properties. He explained how ancient civilisations were obsessed with certain numbers and used them in building and art. He showed how certain numbers keep cropping up in nature and how some mathematicians thought each number had a personality of its own.

'Look at yourselves, there are five of you. Five is an important number – we have five senses, there are five continents, five rings on the Olympic flag, five fingers on each hand. In some cultures the number five is revered because it symbolises the four limbs and the head the controls them.

'Our classes will not be about 'five multiplied by four equals twenty'. We will look at numbers and find the fun, interesting and useful things we can do with them and the magic they bring to the world.'

The five students were still buzzing about Maths when they got back to their living quarters. In the boys' room they were starting to get on a lot better after the dispute over the shower had been solved. Craig and Ajit were watching YouTube videos of soccer bloopers together, and Joe was lying on his bed reading a novel about a schools' rugby player.

Kim knocked on the door and popped her head inside. 'Hello, boys, me and Jess were thinking of asking Luce could we see the cliff room that Joe was in. I miss seeing the sun, it's like being in prison.'

Joe laughed. 'Well, she did offer to give us a tour of the off-limits areas so it's worth asking. You two want to come along?'

Ajit grunted, engrossed in the video clips. Craig shook his head too, afraid he'd miss another hilarious own goal.

Joe joined the girls in the corridor. 'I wonder where Luce is now?' he wondered. 'I was with her in the security office a while ago.'

'She told us to push this button if we needed her,' suggested Jess, pointing at her watch.

'I thought that was in case of emergency only,' frowned Kim.

'Well…' grinned Joe. 'I could say I needed to see the windows room again to help me remember what I saw.'

Jess pushed the button, and Luce's face instantly appeared on the screen.

'What can I do for you, Jess?' she asked.

'Kim and I would like to see the windows room – we haven't seen sunlight for days,' she explained.

'I understand,' Luce replied. 'Stay where you are and I'll

be down to you in two minutes.'

'Hmmm, impressive,' said Kim. 'Don't tell the other lads or they'll be getting her to go out for pizza.'

Luce arrived and showed them to an elevator, which whisked them high into the cliffs that lay on the island's north face. She stepped out and ushered them along to the room that Joe had visited the previous night.

'It's still bright now,' he explained. 'All I could see last night was darkness and the waves crashing below. And, of course, the lights from whatever that was.'

Luce smiled weakly. The girls peered out the windows at the vast ocean that stretched out as far as they could see.

'It's so big, isn't it,' said Jess. 'You just can't see anything else except the sea and the sky.'

Joe screwed up his eyes, trying to focus on the corner of the sky where he had seen the lights, but there was nothing to be seen.

'How long has this island been in existence?' Kim asked Luce.

'Well, I am the second manager of Atlantis,' she started. 'I've been here seventeen years now, and my predecessor was here for seven. The first of our intake are coming up to retirement age now, in most sports, although our chess player could keep going for many years yet.'

'Chess?' asked Jess. 'That's not very sporty…'

'You would be surprised,' replied Luce. 'You need to be physically fit to maintain that level of concentration for so long. And the training your brain receives in playing chess can be of great benefit for those sports where tactics are important. Chess is on the curriculum in Atlantis Academy – one of our second-intake students learned to play here, and he's now a grandmaster. That's a very big deal in chess.'

Joe studied the horizon, scanning back and forth trying to see something out of place. It was impossible to pick out anything in the rough ocean swell, but he had the same uneasy feeling he had the night before and was sure those lights would reappear as soon as night fell.

'It's starting to get dark,' said Kim. 'If there's any lights out there we'll be able to see them better in the darkness.'

Luce looked concerned at this observation and decided to end the visit.

'All right now, we've seen enough here, time to get back for your evening meal.'

'But that's not for another half-hour!' said Jess.

'Yes, but you'll need to wash, and … and maybe change. Yes, that's it… change. You're meeting the captain tonight, so you'll need to wear something more suitable than your tracksuits.'

CHAPTER 19

Joe was annoyed that Luce had cut their visit short, but he decided not to mention it again. When they got back to their rooms they found an envelope on each pillow containing an invitation to dine with the captain that evening.

'She works quickly,' thought Joe.

Craig and Ajit had tired of the stream of bloopers and were each stretched out on their beds reading magazines.

'Do you really think you could be the best tennis player your age in the world when we're finished here?' asked Ajit.

'No, but I think we've a great chance to improve ourselves here. I know how good, or bad, I am, and can't imagine being even the best in my club. But I suppose they've been doing this for years and have had some amazing players here, so they must have good coaches.'

'I suppose so,' agreed Ajit, 'it's just so hard to get your head around it. Like, they've brought me here just because I hit one amazing shot – a total fluke. I'd love to be half-good at one sport, let alone the best at two.'

Joe chipped in. 'I think we have to trust that they know what they're doing. They've spent millions, maybe billions on this place and you just have to look at the wall of fame to see what the results are.'

The dinner turned out to be pretty boring – the captain spent most of the time explaining how the giant submarine-disguised-as-an-island worked, which went way over the heads of most of the students. As far as Joe understood, the whole man-made island was a giant solar panel, and the power it gathered was stored in huge batteries. They needed to surface every few days to soak up more of the sun's rays, but he promised there would be no shortage of that in their next stop.

Later, in bed, Joe tossed and turned, thinking about the mysterious lights he had seen the night before, but not keen to get into any more trouble with Luce. He had been so excited and overawed by his first impressions of the island he had forgotten all about his old life and the family he had left behind. But as the novelty wore off, and his room-mates started squabbling and Luce started laying down the law, he suddenly started feeling homesick.

He was bored by the testing and measuring, and while he was prepared to give the gymnastics a go, what he wanted more than anything was to kick a football again. And kick it hard.

CHAPTER 20

Joe got his wish a lot quicker even than he had hoped. The gymnastics session was brilliant, once you got used to balancing on a narrow wooden plank in a moving submarine island. But the floor was cushioned so nobody did themselves any harm.

The coach, Anna, told them that some of the toughest sports-people she had ever met were gymnasts, and that they trained their bodies to be both hard and flexible – able to withstand enormous pressures, but also able to move quickly and gracefully.

'This is the very best sport for boys and girls who want to be good at other sports,' she explained. 'Every day you are on this island, and for long after you leave it, you should practise some of the drills I am going to show you. It will stand to you.'

Anna was always encouraging and positive, and the morning flew by as they stretched, tumbled, balanced and cavorted. She taught them the safest way to fall, and how to roll head over heels and spring back instantly into action. Every drill was accompanied with a suggestion how each could be worked into other sports.

'That was fantastic,' said Craig as he towelled the sweat out of his hair. 'I didn't think gymnastics could be so tough.'

After lunch Luce introduced them to another new coach, although this one looked nothing like a sportsman. He was much older than the other adults on the island, with long grey hair tied in a ponytail, and small, round glasses. He wasn't wearing one of the brightly-coloured tracksuits either, instead he wore a tweed suit, which clashed horrendously with a pair of expensive gold trainers he wore on his feet.

'My name is Professor Kossuth,' he started, 'and I am going to coach you in football, particularly in one important aspect of football. My speciality is association football, although you will find application for my theories in rugby, Australian, Gaelic, Canadian and American types of football too.

'My life's work has been on the mechanics of kicking a ball. There are fascinating physical forces at work and my theories will help you kick the ball harder and faster, thus giving you those extra micro-seconds needed to beat even the best goalkeepers.'

He started to explain the forces that were involved in just kicking a ball, but Joe's brain just fogged over as the professor started to draw equations on the whiteboard. He listened out for the words, choosing to ignore the numbers, and learned that the surface of a soccer ball goes flat for one-hundredth of a second when a foot connects with it.

The professor posed the students a question: 'Right, who kicks the ball faster, a person who is big and tall, or a small, short person?'

Jess's hand shot up. 'The tall person. Their legs are longer, so they would get a bigger swing.'

The professor smiled and wiped the whiteboard clean. He scribbled away for a minute or so before addressing the class.

'This formula shows the velocity of a 20 metres-per second kick by an adult who weighs 100kg, and this shows that for a 60kg person. The bigger person's kick results in the ball travelling at a velocity of 32.7 metres per second, while the shorter player's kick is 31.9.'

'But in the real world those two players would not kick at the same velocity as their legs would weigh differently. So the smaller player, putting in the same effort, would have a higher leg velocity.

'However, if the short player's leg velocity were to get up to 28 metres per second, the ball would shoot off at 45 metres per second, a huge increase over the taller player.

'And that is why, rather than trying to bulk you up, we will be working on increasing your leg speed…'

The students were a bit stunned by the professor's conclusions – at least those who could understand them – but he continued with his theories.

'One thing that always irritates me watching football is the player who kicks with a huge follow-through. What you must remember is that the follow-through adds nothing to the velocity of the kick – the ball has already gone so that energy is wasted.

'We must concentrate on getting you into a position so you use as much energy as you can on that one-hundredth of a second when you actually make contact with the ball, not on what comes after. Although kicking without some follow-through is impossible, of course.'

The professor explained a few more of his theories, but said he would save the explanations for another day.

'I can see a lot of this is very difficult for you to understand, as you don't begin to study physics in school until you are two or three years older. But I will try to keep it simple and show you how to put these ideas into practice.'

He brought the group down the corridor to a room covered with an artificial grass surface. He took a sack of footballs out of the cupboard and tossed one to each of the kids.

'Joe, you are the one who came here as the soccer player. You show us all how best to kick the ball.'

Joe gulped. He placed the ball on ground and steadied himself into a comfortable position. He swung his left leg back and smacked the ball as best he could.

'Not bad at all,' said the Professor. 'You have kicked with the correct part of your foot and made contact with the correct area of the ball, and they are two of the most important points. But your head position was all wrong, and the angle with which you swung your leg. If that were a match and you were standing on the penalty spot, that shot would go approximately one-point-three metres wide…'

CHAPTER 21

Joe was fascinated by what Professor Kossuth had taught them, and after lessons were over for the day he returned to the practice room to test out everything he had learned.

He liked the feel of kicking a soccer ball again, and it reminded him of home, and the countless hours he spent doing the same thing against the back wall. He thought about his mum and dad and how much he missed them. The house would be a quieter place now, especially with no-one smacking a ball off the wall.

He was disturbed from his daydream by a knock on the door, followed by Luce popped her head inside.

'Great to see you putting the Professor's theories into practice,' she grinned. 'But you really need to come to the canteen for dinner. We're going on an adventure as soon as you've eaten.'

Joe followed Luce to where the rest of his friends were already tucking into a tasty pasta dish.

'Hurry up, Joe,' urged Ajit. 'The captain says we can come to join him on the bridge as soon as dinner is over.'

Joe hated rushing food, but his friends all stared at him as he chewed every morsel. When he had eaten about half his meal he pushed the plate away, saying he wasn't hungry.

The four others rushed out the door, followed by Joe who had detoured to the buffet to pocket an energy bar for later.

'I wonder are we under water or on the surface?' mused Kim as they waited outside the door of the bridge, from where the submarine was run.

'I think we're submerged,' said Craig. 'It's always runs a tiny bit smoother when we're under water.'

Joe shrugged. 'I never notice either way. It's amazing how little you can feel the island moving.'

As soon as Luce joined them the door opened and a man in a uniform answered.

'Ah, the students. Come in, come in, you're just in time to see the really fun part of this job.'

'I hope it's more fun than his efforts at dinner last night,' whispered Kim.

Joe and Jess struggled to fight back their sniggers, and Luce gave them a dirty look.

'Right,' she snapped. 'Please sit down on this bench here and remain quiet. The captain and his team have an important job to do and need to devote their full concentration. He will talk to you when he decides it is necessary, so no questions until the end.'

And with that she sat down, and the five children followed her. It was only then that Joe got a chance to take in what was in the room – mostly screens and control panels – but he suddenly felt over-powered by the giant window that covered one wall. Joe stared at it, and realised they were definitely underwater and the island was moving past a shoal of fish.

'Whoooa!' he gasped. 'It looks like a giant fish tank!'

'Except we're the tiny things looking out, and that's the vast ocean looking in at us,' smiled the captain.

The students were transfixed by the mysterious world outside the window and pointed out the different sea creatures to each other as they drifted past.

'We are now approximately fifteen kilometres off the north coast of Barbados, which is in the Caribbean Sea, and we intend to surface shortly. We will stay a good distance off-shore, but we have several good friends on Barbados who will ensure our stay is safe and we can restock supplies. We will also be taking on a new member of staff, who Luce can tell you about.'

'Yes, I suppose this is as good a time as any to tell you. We've been studying Ajit's numbers and we reckon he could be as good a bowler as a batsman in cricket. And as an all-rounder is a particularly valuable member of a team we have decided to recruit a coaching specialist from the home of the great West Indies batsmen and fast-bowlers. You may not recognise this gentleman, Ajit, but your father surely will.

'We won't be concentrating on your cricket for a while yet Ajit, maybe not till next year, but the rest of you will get a chance to learn the game and work on some skills. And there's no better place to do that than under a Caribbean sun.'

The captain raised his arm. 'Thank you, Luce. And now I will ask you all to resume your seats and hold on to the arm rests in case you get thrown about on surfacing.'

The children all sat back down and held on as the island rose through the water.

'Here we are, we're fifty metres from the surface,' said the captain, pointing at a counter upon which the number was getting smaller by the second.

The water was rushing past the window, and a couple of fish came up close to the glass as Joe watched the counter race past 25… 20… 15….

'Hold tight!' called the captain, as the island began to lurch in the waves. The top of the cliffs broke the surface first, and those looking out the window just below it got a good view of the dramatic scene as the water rushed away and the cliffs shot into the air above the blue Caribbean.

Joe waited until the island had stopped surfacing before stepping over to view their new location. The cliffs were facing north, away from Barbados, but he was able to see the island on the screens thanks to cameras which were pointed in its direction.

He was astonished at how blue the sea looked; the sky was an even more vivid shade of the colour.

'How long are we staying here?' Craig asked Luce.

'Perhaps three or four days. We have maintenance to do, and we need to restock our larder. But as it is such a beautiful place it would be good for you to get outdoors and recharge your own batteries and stocks of Vitamin D.'

'Cool,' grinned Jess. 'When we were on the boat in the middle of the night in Clew Bay last week, the last place I thought we were going was a Caribbean sun holiday.'

'The bad news, however, is that it is almost sundown and you won't have time for a swim before night falls. So, dig your swimsuits out of the wardrobe and have them all set for tomorrow. You will have classes as normal in the morning, but you can take the afternoon off…'

The kids cheered wildly as they left the room.

'This is like when it snows at home and they give us a day off school,' grinned Joe.

'Only now we don't have to sit indoors shivering and watching cartoons on TV,' laughed Jess.

CHAPTER 22

'**I** know we're getting a half-day, but it's a real pain to be stuck in here listening to Professor Kossuth when the sun is beating down outside,' grumped Craig over breakfast.

'He sent a message saying we were to wear game kit, so I suppose we're in the practice room?' said Kim.

Joe shrugged, finished off his carrot juice, and stood up.

'Well I'm going to be first in line to test the speed gun on my kick. I reckon I have upped it by a couple of extra metres,' he grinned.

But there would be no speed gun for Joe this morning, as the Professor was standing outside the practice room wearing an even more outlandish costume than before. His tweed suit had been replaced by a loud check shirt with the sleeves cut off, and orange shorts which stretched down to his knees, while his golden sneakers had been discarded in favour of old-style football ankle boots, which had also been painted gold.

'Well boys and girls,' he smiled, 'while the astroturf in the practice room is a perfectly acceptable surface to play on while we are whizzing about the oceans, there is no real substitute for a kickabout outdoors. So, we are going to take this morning's practical on the grass pitch on the roof of Atlantis, which means you will need your outdoor boots.'

The five cheered and rushed off to change their footwear. They were starting to get irritated at having to spend all their time cooped up indoors, so the chance to get some fresh air, especially in a nice climate, was exciting.

'I can't wait to see the sky again,' grinned Jess as they waited.

Kalvin came and hauled back the enormous bolts on two sets of doors to enter the cottage before twisting his key in the lock and pushing the final door open. In flooded the brightest sunlight Joe had ever seen.

'Oh yes, before you go anywhere you will have to wear these sunglasses,' called out Luce, who handed them each a pair of wraparound shades, which had an elastic strap to hold them in place on their head. 'You've been indoors for so long that your eyes will need to get used to the glare.'

The five took slow, careful steps out on to the island,

which was now surrounded by a beautiful blue ocean.

'It's completely dry, too,' announced Kim. 'The sun must have burnt off the water after we surfaced.'

Joe knelt to test the grass, which felt just like ordinary grass although a lighter colour than he remembered from Clew Bay. The ground, too, felt the same as on the pitches back home.

'Yes, Joe,' grinned the Professor. 'It's also artificial – it would be impossible to grow ordinary grass when we spend so much time underwater. But this is a far more advanced version than the astroturf you are used to, or indeed than we have inside.

'This is the only place on earth – outside Victor's laboratories – that you will find this surface. Not only does it have to be suitable to play on, but it must also blend in with the colour of grass in whatever region of the world we drop anchor. And, of course, it must be resistant to the salty water of the deep ocean.'

Kalvin stepped out from behind them. 'I almost forgot,' he said, before pushing a button on his console at which a cluster of palm trees shot up from the ground beside the cottage. 'All part of the camouflage,' he chuckled.

'Off you run,' the friendly giant suggested. 'But stay away from the goalmouths for a minute.'

Joe picked up one of the balls that Professor Kossuth had dropped, and began to dribble with it out towards the lower shore of the island.

'What does he mean by "goalmouths"?' wondered Kim.

'I suppose this bit of the island is roughly the shape of a pitch,' suggested Ajit.

'Look...' called Craig, as the distinctive shape of a football goal slowly emerged from the ground, sliding into the air until it reached the appropriate height.

'There's one at the other end too,' pointed out Jess.

Kalvin grinned and waved his console. 'It's all here in my magic box of tricks,' he laughed, before flicking another switch which saw strips of grass change colour so that the full pitch markings were set out in white.

The Professor led the astonished students towards the penalty spot closest to the cottage. Again, Kalvin fiddled with his magic box and a netting fence emerged from the ground, behind the goal, and climbed into the air until it towered over them from a height of fifteen metres.

'That's just in case any of you don't hit the target,' chuckled the professor.

'What happens if the ball rebounds off the bar and goes out over the side,' asked Craig.

'Well… we'll have to wait and see if that happens,' replied Kalvin. 'I may decide to throw you overboard to get the ball back.'

The Professor asked the five to take three shots at goal each – Kalvin stood in as goalkeeper and even though he moved slowly it still wasn't easy to get the ball past him.

Professor Kossuth took note of where their shots ended up, and then went step by step through his theory of kicking a football, asking the kids to copy them very slowly.

It was a bit like playing soccer in slow-motion, thought Joe, although the drill forced you to think about every movement you made. Once they had mastered the steps, they were asked to speed it up slightly, and later still to do it at normal speed.

The students weren't new to football, as they all played a little in parks or gardens at home, but they still found that they were much more accurate and powerful than they had been when they took their first kicks, and most of their shots were now on target. Jess surprised even herself by never once missing the goal.

As the morning wound down, the Professor had a suggestion.

'All right, let us finish off the session with a little match…'

'We could have the three boys playing against Kalvin and the girls, with you as referee,' suggested Ajit.

'No, no, no,' grinned the Professor. 'That would be very unfair, and besides, I want a game too.'

'Then you could join the girls and Kalvin could ref?' offered Craig.

'No. Kalvin and I will take on the rest of you. We will try our best in the first half and, as I expect us to be at least 5-0 up, we will take it easy for the second…'

CHAPTER 23

Craig snorted. '5-0! You've got to be joking. Sure, Kalvin can't run very quickly.'

'Kalvin won't need to run quickly. He will be playing in goal and I will be the outfield player. To give you a chance I will lower the crossbar on your goal by one metre too,' signalling to Kalvin who made the adjustment on his console.

'And we will play fifteen minutes each way,' finished the Professor as he went through a series of pre-match exercises and stretches.

Joe got the rest of the team together. 'This has *got* to be a joke,' sniffed Craig. 'One old guy in golden boots and Frankenstein in goal. We'll murder them.'

'I'm not so sure,' said Kim. 'We're not exactly world-beaters at football ourselves. And how do you think he got to be a soccer coach anyway?'

'You play in goal, Craig,' suggested Joe. 'You're the tallest and are used to diving in tennis.'

Craig shrugged. 'OK. But if I don't get to touch the ball in the first half I want to come out for the second.'

The teams lined up – Joe put himself at the back of a diamond formation, with Jess up front, and Ajit and Kim on the wings – before Luce, who had come back outside at the professor's request, blew the whistle for the game to start.

Jess first tapped the ball to Ajit who set off on a run. The professor seemed happy to let him do so and moved inside to mark Kim.

Kalvin came out towards Ajit, reducing the area he had to shoot at, but Ajit responded by passing the ball to his left where he had spotted Joe running into space. With all he had learned from the Professor over the previous day running through his head, Joe gathered the ball, pushed it a little wide and forward, and lifted his left leg. He connected with the ball perfectly and watched as it sailed towards the top corner of the net.

Joe had already half-turned to go back to half-way for the restart when Kalvin, previously a lumbering giant, executed a move that would have been hard even for whatever weird-looking creature would result from a cross between a cheetah and a salmon. The doorkeeper raced across the box, leaping high in the air and stretching his enormous arm out.

He extended his fingers fully and arched his back in time to tip the ball just over the crossbar.

Joe, and the rest of his team-mates, were stunned.

'How did he…?' gasped Kim.

Kalvin unleashed an enormous grin. 'So, who says I'm too slow?' he laughed.

Joe ran to collect the ball and take the corner kick. He checked which of his team was the best positioned to receive a pass.

He was astonished to see the Professor was actually standing on the half-way line, not bothering to help out in defence.

Joe swung the ball into the penalty area, where it fell nicely to Ajit, who took the ball right up to Kalvin before side-footing it to Jess.

The little striker rushed in and placed it as far away from Kalvin as she could, but again the giant doorkeeper was able to up his pace and dive across the goal to collect the ball.

'Hard luck, Jess,' called Joe. 'You'll beat him next time.'

Kalvin walked out to the end of his area with the ball at his feet before picking it up. He bounced the ball twice, all the while watching the professor, who was being marked closely by Joe and Ajit.

He rolled the ball towards the group, and the Professor came out to meet it. Joe went across him to tackle, but was surprised when the ball disappeared from view and was next seen behind the Professor.

'How did you do that?' he asked.

'Always watch my feet,' laughed the professor.

The aged academic skipped past Jess and zeroed in on the goal. Ajit tried to tackle him, but again was too slow for his tricky feet.

The Professor paused for half a second, looking at Craig and the goal he was defending. He seemed to be making calculations in his head, before gently lifting his right foot and whipping it across the ball, which looped into the air over Craig before zipping down and past him into the net.

'How did he do that?' complained Craig. 'That's black magic, that is.'

Joe winced at his team-mate's childish behaviour and told him to get the ball back to Kim who was ready to kick-off.

The Professor smiled and trotted back to half-way. Kim rolled the ball to Ajit, who was stunned to see that the Professor had suddenly accelerated into a sprint and stolen the ball off his toes.

Again, the elderly gentleman ran like someone a quarter of his age, dropping his shoulder and swerving past Joe before firing a ball along the ground at such a speed that Craig had no chance of getting down to stop it.

'That's 2-0 and we're only playing three minutes,' complained Jess as she met Joe at half-way. 'The old man is unbelievable.'

'Maybe he's not as old as he looks, or maybe he just eats a lot of that beetroot and hummus that Luce is always pushing on us.'

The rest of the first half followed a similar pattern, with the youngsters struggling to catch the sprightly soccer coach, and whenever they got a chance to shoot there was the giant doorkeeper barring their way to goal.

As half-time approached, and Craig was collecting the ball from his net for the fifth time, he asked the Professor a question about something that had been bugging him all through the half.

'Hey, Professor,' he called. 'Why is there a long net to stop the ball at your end, and nothing at this end.'

Professor Kossuth looked puzzled at first, but then smiled.

'Why, of course we don't need a net behind that goal. Sure, I have never once had a shot off-target in almost twenty years...'

CHAPTER 24

The five students sat on the grass for the half-time break, guzzling bottles of water that Kelly had thoughtfully brought out to them.

'That was unbelievable,' said Kim. 'He's so fit, and so fast.'

They stared across at the Professor, who was spending the interval doing push-ups and stretches.

'His shots are amazing,' said Joe. 'He seems to line them up for a split-second and has it all worked out to the nearest centimetre. I don't think there's any way we can stop him scoring if he gets to shoot. So, we should try to stop him shooting.'

'That's easier said than done, Joe,' said Ajit. 'He's stronger than you'd think and once he has the ball at his feet it's like it's stuck there on the end of a piece of string.'

'Maybe so, but I have a plan,' replied Joe.

'Would you like to change ends for the second half?' asked Luce. 'Obviously we should do it, but if you guys are kicking into the sea-end goal there may be some "balls overboard".'

Craig frowned. 'We'll play into the sea goal, thank you. And we won't need any nets.'

'All right,' said Luce, 'but remember the rule. If you kick it into the ocean you swim after it.'

The Professor kicked off the second half, although he didn't have anyone to kick it to, so he was – strictly speaking – breaking the rules.

The four student outfield players had decided their best chance was to surround the Professor and prevent him going anywhere with the ball. They each took a position on the compass and refused to let him past, with the two nearest also ready to cover.

The Professor was intrigued by their tactics and found it quite a challenge. He tried everything – flicking the ball in the air to try to distract them, pushing the ball through a gap, back-heeling the ball and trying to recover it by running backwards – but each time the children recovered and again locked him in their trap.

'Bravo,' he called out, after three or four minutes of play going around in circles. 'This is a very shrewd manoeuvre and may even work in a short game such as we are playing. But remember it is a very warm day and you will tire yourselves out very quickly playing such tactics. But, for now, you have mastered me.'

And with that, the Professor passed the ball straight to Jess, who needed no encouragement to hare away towards the goal. The young striker moved to fire the ball to Kalvin's right, but shifted at the last second and rammed it hard to his left.

Jess knew Kalvin was a lot faster than he had seemed at first, but this time he was just late enough reacting to her switch to give her a chance. The ball thundered off the inside of the post and bounced into the net.

Jess was swamped by her team-mates, even Craig, who had run the length of the pitch to add his congratulations.

'OK, OK, let's get back playing,' she urged. 'We're still 5-1 down.'

The Professor was itching to restart the game, but waited for his young opponents to get back in position. He tipped off, immediately making a run in on goal, and was about to unleash a kick when Joe came in from the side, flicked the ball off the Professor's toe and side-footed it up-field.

This time it was the turn of Ajit to collect the ball, but the youngster this time hared off in the direction of the corner flag with his yellow shirt blazing in the sun. Kalvin was puzzled by this and made to follow the attacker.

He left just enough space for Ajit to thunder the ball past him into the penalty area where Kim came rushing in to control the ball and place it, with the side of her foot, in the empty net.

'Two,' screamed Craig. 'Come on now, Atlantis United, we have these old guys on the run.'

But try as they might, the young fivesome just couldn't create any more chances to score. Luce told Craig that there was less than half a minute left to play when he gathered the ball and shaped to kick it up the field.

The goalkeeper spotted that his opposite man had come up to the edge of his penalty box to call some instruction out to the Professor, so Craig decided to take advantage.

He dropped the ball on to his right foot and kicked it as hard as he could. The ball landed about five metres in front of Kalvin and bounced over his head. The giant goalie realised what was happening and worked out that the ball wasn't moving fast enough. He raced back three or four strides before diving straight at the ball. It was just a metre or two from the goal when he connected with his huge, clenched fist.

'Oh no,' called Joe, as the ball flew up in the air. The players all watched as it climbed into the sky, eight, nine, ten metres up, and started to descend.

Kalvin got back on to his line in case the ball dropped back into play, but he needn't have worried. The ball finally landed on the crossbar, took another bounce into the air, and fell into the Caribbean Sea.

'Tee hee, that's Craig going for a swim so,' chuckled the Professor.

'No way!' replied the goalkeeper. 'My shot was on target – it was Kalvin who knocked it into the ocean.'

Luce strode to the edge of the island and looked out to sea, where the ball was bobbing slowly away.

'I think Craig is right, Kalvin, it was your fault, so you must retrieve the ball,' she said.

Craig had a huge grin on his face.

'I'm looking forward to seeing that big lad getting his feet wet,' he chuckled as his exhausted team-mates sat around on the grass, delighted that the game was over.

But Kalvin had the last laugh. Out of the pocket of his enormous overcoat he lifted the console and twisted one of the knobs as he pointed at the ball, bobbing in the sea. The ball shot up in the air and flew, as if it had wings, all the way back to the island. It dropped at the feet of Kalvin who, with a flick, passed it to Craig.

'No way,' complained Craig. 'I hope you would have told him to use that controller if I had kicked it out.'

'Maybe,' smiled Luce. 'Maybe not.'

CHAPTER 25

The students enjoyed their afternoon off, lazing around in the sun and taking dips in the warm sea. Jess and Craig were the strongest swimmers and had races out to a football that Kalvin had helpfully kicked into the water.

Swimming off Atlantis was a bit different to a normal island as there was no beach, and no shallows to paddle in. It was like jumping into a giant swimming pool that only had a deep end, so the other three, being less confident swimmers, stayed close to shore.

Joe got bored splashing around after a while and decided to explore the island that he had only seen briefly on that first morning in Clew Bay. Jess and Craig were still twenty metres out to sea, and Ajit and Kim were playing water-polo with another of the footballs, so he wandered off on his own.

'Be careful if you go up near the cliffs, Joe,' called Kalvin, who seemed to be acting as their life guard-cum-babysitter for the afternoon.

'I will,' called Joe, as he set off at a trot up the slope which gradually steepened as it neared the top. He turned and looked back down at the island and marvelled at the idea of creating an occasionally-submarine artificial island that could have a football pitch on its roof.

'Victor's obviously a genius, and a brilliant businessman, but he's also a bit mad,' he chuckled to himself.

He walked the last few steps to the top of the island, taking Kalvin's advice and steering clear of the cliff edge. He sat down and gazed out at the ocean and pinched himself, as he had done several times since he had come to Atlantis Island.

'The lads back in Woodstock are probably hugging them-selves to keep warm, training out in the wind and the rain while I'm lazing around in the Caribbean,' he thought. 'They probably don't miss me at all – on the pitch anyway – and Robbie's still wondering when he's going to get a call from that scout.'

He closed his eyes and thought back to home, and all the things he missed. He didn't want to feel too homesick, but he enjoyed thinking about his mum's shepherd's pie, and what might be happening on his favourite TV zombie show.

Being tired from his efforts in the football match, and nice and warm from the sun, Joe soon dozed off, where he continued to dream of undead monsters who devoured meat and potato pies.

'Joe! Are you all right,' came the call that woke him up. It was Kalvin at the bottom of the hill. The other four kids were out of the water, wrapped in towels, and standing next to the cottage. It was also quite a bit darker, and he saw the blazing sun had turned bright red and was hovering just above the horizon.

'It gets dark very quickly here,' called Kalvin, 'Get down here and we'll head inside for food.'

Joe stood up and took one last look over the top of the cliffs where he was astonished to see the same flickering lights he had seen the week before.

'Kalvin,' he called out, 'Those lights are here again, can you get Luce to come up here quickly?'

The giant pushed a button on his pager and Luce and two other Atlantis crew emerged out through the door of the cottage within thirty seconds.

'It's Joe – he's seen it again,' Kalvin told them as they rushed up the slope.

The youngster pointed out to where he had seen the strange flickering in the dusk sky.

'Yes, I see it too,' said Luce. 'OK, Joe, you go straight down below please. Now.'

The Atlantis manager stared at the sky before taking a small pair of binoculars out of her pocket and peering closely at the lights.

'Right, Kalvin, we need to submerge, and quickly. Can you tidy away those goals and let's get the show on the road. I'll go straight to the bridge but we need to be under water in five minutes – max.'

CHAPTER 26

Atlantis sank beneath the waves four minutes and twenty-three seconds later, by which time Joe, Craig and Ajit were back in their quarters. They were all a bit rattled by what had happened and Craig and Ajit renewed their squabble about whose turn it was to have a shower.

Joe decided to leave them to it and lay back on his pillow. Something was annoying him about the last few moments on the cliff-top, but he couldn't put his finger on it. He flicked through a magazine and tried to ignore Craig and Ajit.

Ajit came out of the shower first and sat on the edge of his bed, towelling his hair.

'So, it was those funny lights again, Joe? What do you think they are?'

'I don't know, Aj, I haven't a clue but Luce seems to be worried about them...'

Joe stopped. He had called the lights 'them,' but Kalvin and Luce had called them 'it'. They must know what it is.

He explained this to Ajit.

'Do you think it is some sort of plane following us?' wondered Joe. 'It's a bit low in the sky to be a satellite, and too high to be a ship.'

'It could be something like a drone,' suggested Ajit. 'Though it must have some powerful battery to follow us across the Atlantic.'

'Maybe there's a ship following it and recharging the batteries,' wondered Joe. 'Or two drones taking turns.'

'Or maybe it's like the whole island and has a little solar panel?' added Ajit.

Once Joe had finished his shower he dressed quickly in his black tracksuit and went to find Luce. She was on the bridge with the captain, so Joe knocked and waited for her to open the door.

He could hear raised voices, angry voices, before Luce finally came to answer Joe's knock.

'What is it?' she snapped.

'Do you know what the lights are?' he replied.

Luce paused before answering. 'We have an idea.'

'Is it a drone?' asked Joe.

'Why do you suspect that?' asked Luce, who had turned

away from Joe.

'Because you called the lights "it", not "them",' he told her.

Luce stared back at Joe and shrugged.

'That's very clever of you. And yes, we do think it is a drone. However, some sort of electronic masking has been used that stops our radar seeing it. It's very worrying because it shows whoever is following us has some very slick technology, and therefore plenty of money.

'Can you keep this from your classmates, please, I don't want them to panic and think they are in danger.'

'Well, I don't know...' started Joe, carefully, '*are* we in danger? Ajit was the one who came up with the idea that it might be a drone, and I think they all deserve to be told what's going on. No one will panic.'

Luce stared back at Joe.

'I ... I suppose you're right about needing to tell them. But we don't really know much about the drones ourselves. I'll talk to the captain and I'll call down to you in half an hour when you're at dinner. But please say nothing until then.'

Joe left the bridge and spent the next thirty minutes avoiding Ajit. He wandered into the practice room and decided to try out the rugby set-up. He had never played the sport before although he had enjoyed watching it on television and reckoned he might even be better at it than he was at football – but he loved football too much to give it up.

There were a few drills that Kelly had taught them that he enjoyed, including passing to a hologram player who called out your mark out of five once he had 'caught' the ball, and a type of darts for line-out throwers which also registered your score against the computer. Joe had checked into the room using his swipe-card so all his scores would be recorded in his file. It was a good way of checking how you were progressing in each sport or activity.

He got a bleep on his watch telling him it was dinner time, so he tidied up and rambled down to the canteen. The other four were already tucking in.

'Hey, Joe, what happened to you? Did you get to talk to Luce?' asked Ajit.

Joe just shrugged. 'I did, and she's going to come down to talk to us in a few minutes…'

'So, what's she going to tell us?' asked Kim.

'What are those lights?' asked Jess.

Joe held up his hands. 'Sorry, sorry, l really don't know

what exactly she's going to tell us, but I think she will say that we're being followed.'

CHAPTER 27

The rest of Joe's classmates were a bit stunned by his suggestion and were still chatting about it in loud voices when Luce came through the door five minutes later.

She raised her right hand in greeting – and to call them to silence.

'OK, class, I apologise for the quick change of plan and our dramatic departure from Barbados. This was because Joe here spotted lights in the sky which we now believe are part of a drone which had been following us for some time. We are confused because there is no way of tracking us underwater and yet it keeps cropping up when we surface, so we will investigate that further. But we are no wiser as to why it is following us.

'We do have our suspicions, however. You understand that you are here to avail of the most modern techniques of sports science, nutrition, training and technology. We hope we can apply these to turn you five into brilliant sports professionals, capable of anything with your minds and bodies in your chosen field.

'But that sort of information is highly sought after. Sport is such a lucrative business that there are governments, top sports clubs and sports kit manufacturers who would pay millions to get inside this facility and study what we are up to. And we know that some of these people will go beyond the law to do so.

'We had some information that someone would attempt to infiltrate the voyage across to Leap Island, but we put some plans in place to prevent that. I understand Craig's taxi was followed, but wasn't intercepted?'

Craig nodded. 'The taxi driver turned off his lights and shook him off. But it was a bit hairy for a while.'

'Well, we aren't sure who is behind this, but we fear they have been able to plant something on the island that acts as a beacon for some sort of tracking device, which is either in this mysterious drone, or in some ship following it.'

Kim put up her hand to ask a question. 'But are we in any danger? Are they going to sink the island?'

'I'm sure you won't be in any danger,' replied Luce. 'Whoever is doing this is looking to copy or steal our methods.

The five looked at each other. There wasn't any panic, but

they were all very concerned.

'Can we go home?' asked Jess.

'It would be more dangerous to try to get you to an international airport,' Luce replied. 'We are in no danger under water, and we will be trying to find out how they are following us. Stay calm and keep working away, we'll talk to Victor and see if we have to make decisions like that at the right time.

'The captain has a plan to hide out for a while at a quiet island he knows in the Caribbean – we have to link up with Deryck, the cricket coach who we were supposed to collect in Barbados. It's about two hundred kilometres away, so we'll be there by morning.

'I suggest you get some sleep, and please don't worry, we have everything in hand,' said Luce before she left the canteen.

The five were very rattled by the developments and had little appetite for the rest of their meal.

As he toyed with the food, Craig turned to Jess. 'Were you serious about wanting to go home?'

'Well, yes,' she replied. 'I'm not hanging around here to get shot at by criminals or whoever it is. This is scary.'

'I don't think there's much chance of us getting shot,' said Joe. 'We seem well protected here and they were able to get the whole island under water in a couple of minutes.'

'Well, I wish they'd find out what it was that keeps that drone thing coming after us. It makes me very nervous,' said Jess.

CHAPTER 28

Few of the children slept well that night. The submarine was travelling at top speed so the hum of the engines was noticeable and Joe, for one, couldn't get the image of the drone out of his mind.

He woke to a bleep from his watch telling him he would have classes as normal, with the tennis coach keen to work on their serves. He dragged himself out of bed, knowing full well that he hadn't had nearly enough sleep, and stood under the shower.

The water woke him up and sparked him into action for the day ahead. He dressed quickly and left the dormitory, heading for the spiral staircase that took him up to the room where he had first spotted the drone.

As he reached the staircase, however, he found it was being guarded – by Kalvin.

'Good morning, young Joe, and what has you in this out-of-bounds part of the island?'

'Eh, good morning Kalvin. I was just out for a walk and

wanted to check out that staircase. It's good fun to run up and down it – it really warms up my leg muscles before tennis. There's no other staircase on the island.'

Kalvin looked suspicious. 'Really? Well I suppose there'll be no harm done. Just don't climb out the exit hatch onto the cliffs, won't you?'

Joe nodded, wondering what exit hatch Kalvin was talking about. 'Of course. I'll not be longer than ten minutes up and down,' he added.

Joe raced up the stairs as fast as he could and didn't even stop for breath before he reached the top deck.

'198… 199… 200…' he gasped as he climbed the last step and leaned over the fence to rest. After a few seconds he realised time was short so he scurried along the walkway to the viewing room. Inside he went straight to the windows, realising they had just surfaced as the sunlight flooded the room. He stared down at the waves below before he scanned the skies for any aerial objects.

There was nothing to be seen, so he quickly slipped out of the room and descended the stairs as quick as he safely could.

'198… 199… 200…' he uttered as his feet hit the floor

after he had finished his descent.

Kalvin grinned at him. 'Two hundred up and down, that's some serious step work,' he laughed. 'I would be ready for going back to bed after that. You enjoy your tennis and take it easy,' he added as Joe waved his farewell.

Joe joined the rest of the class in the canteen for breakfast.

'Porridge today, for some reason,' grumbled Craig. 'We're here in the Caribbean where they have lots of fresh fruit and other delicious things and we have to eat grey stodge from home – which looks even more disgusting in a turquoise bowl.'

'Oh, stop being such a grouch, Craig,' laughed Jess. 'Porridge is the breakfast of kings – I bet King Victor eats it anyway. If you didn't daydream in nutrition class you'd realise how good it is for you. All my distance running heroes swear by it.'

'I see you've stopped worrying about the evil criminals following us and have moved onto the important stuff like breakfast,' sniggered Kim.

'Well, whatever about the criminals, the captain has decided we're safe for now. We've just surfaced,' Joe told them, going on to explain his pre-breakfast excursion to the top deck.

'Do you not worry about getting into trouble?' asked Jess.

Joe shrugged. 'I'm usually a bit of a goody-goody to be honest, but I couldn't sleep and wanted to see for myself what was going on. And what's the worst that could happen? They can't expel me – they already said they can't let us off the island and I'd say they'd be afraid we'd sell the secrets. If we could remember what they were.'

The five were silent for the rest of breakfast, each having plenty to think about. Their meal was again interrupted by Luce.

'Good morning, and welcome to Carriacou…'

'Where?' asked Jess, who knew loads about geography, but had never heard of this place.

'Carr-i-a-cou,' said Luce, slowly. 'It's a tiny island in a small island group called the Grenadines. Our captain spent some time here a few years ago and has some friends here who will look after us. We need to do some serious investigation to find if there's something on Atlantis Island that is helping the drone keep up with us.

'You will be leaving the island and spending the day on Carriacou while we complete our search. Kalvin will go with you, but please, please, please don't wander off,' she said, staring at Joe.

'Will we have classes there?' asked Craig.

'No, I'm afraid they don't have the facilities there. Consider it as a mid-term break – I'm told there are beautiful beaches here, and Kalvin will take you to a turtle sanctuary if anyone is interested…'

'Turtles?' said Jess. 'Yes please, I LOVE turtles.'

CHAPTER 29

When the children emerged on to the surface of the island, a dinghy was waiting for them with a very short local sitting at the back.

'I'm Mokie,' he grinned. 'But my friends and enemies call me Mini Moke.'

Kalvin introduced himself and the five students and told him they'd like to go ashore.

'I'll take you to Hillsborough first, that's our capital city,' he said.

The island was anchored close to shore off a quiet bay, overlooked by just one building. The dinghy skipped quickly over the water, which was almost entirely flat, and headed down the coast.

Joe trailed his hand in the crystal-clear water; he could see brightly coloured fish darting below.

'Careful there, big boy,' warned Mokie. 'Those white ones have teeth like razor blades. They'd give your hand a good shave if they got too close.'

Joe snapped his hand out of the water as his classmates laughed.

'And don't get off the main tracks on the island,' suggested Mokie. 'There's plenty of snakes and other beasties in the long grass.'

'This place doesn't sound like a great place to visit when you're trying to stay safe,' sighed Kim.

Mokie steered the dinghy around the headline and made for the harbour wall.

'Welcome to capital city,' he grinned, sweeping his arm across the horizon at a scattering of little more than a hundred one- and two-storey buildings.

'That's not a city!' said Jess.

'It is, it's our capital city,' smiled Mokie. 'We don't have any bigger ones on Carriacou.'

A large black SUV was waiting on the harbour wall, and the party was quickly ushered inside.

'Luce said we weren't to dilly-dally in any public areas,' explained Kalvin. 'So we're going to take you to the turtle sanctuary and later we'll go to a small hotel which Victor has paid to be closed down today and tonight if necessary.'

'Tonight?' asked Kim. 'Does that mean we're staying over?'

'Nothing is confirmed yet,' replied Kalvin. 'My instructions are to take you to the hotel for a meal and then wait for someone to collect us. We've booked out all the rooms just in case there's a delay with the island.'

'What about clothes?' asked Craig. 'We need to change twice a day in this heat and we'll need a change for tomorrow too.'

'Twice a day?' laughed Kalvin. 'You're obviously not doing your own laundry Craig! But don't worry, Mokie is heading out to the island and will collect a change of clothes for the morning – and whatever else Luce decides you need.'

The driver set off through the city, and quickly reached the countryside. Craig and Kim were arguing about something so Joe switched his brain off and took in the surroundings. The sky was as blue as he had ever seen it, but the people seemed to live in shacks.

'We get hit by lots of hurricanes,' said the driver, spotting Joe staring at one basic homestead. 'Lots of homes get wrecked so people live in shanties until they build a new house.'

Joe thought of his own home in a land that didn't have to worry about extreme weather events like this place. He reckoned wind and rain was a small price to pay for that.

The SUV left the road and headed up a track with jungle on each side. This was what Mokie had warned about – Joe had no intention of wandering into these trees and allowing his legs to become a pin cushion for deadly snakes. The track seemed to go on forever – for three or four kilometres anyway – and the group were sore and exhausted from holding tight as the SUV bumped along.

At the end was a small cluster of buildings and steps leading down to the beach. A woman came out to greet them.

'Welcome to our sanctuary,' she smiled, 'I understand you are friends of Mokie, which means you are friends of mine. Come in and make yourselves at home. We have a group of little sea turtles we rescued this morning I'd like you to meet.'

Jess was in heaven, cooing and grinning at the tiny creatures that the woman, Wanda, brought to show them. Joe and Ajit were less impressed but pretended to be interested. Craig and Kim just wandered down to the beach to sit on the hull of an upturned rowing boat.

After a while Joe rambled down to join them and joined in an impromptu gymnastics session where Craig was trying to stand on one hand for as long as he could.

'Impressive, Craig,' smiled Joe. 'You've really taken to the new sports. Anna will be delighted when she sees how far you've come.'

They all tried different exercises, showing off the tricks they'd learned, marvelling at how much fitter and stronger they had got. But they soon tired of it and lay on the sand staring out to sea.

'This is a bit lame, isn't it,' said Kim. 'It's like they're keeping us out of the way.'

'Well, I suppose they need to check everything,' said Joe.

'But surely they checked all that before we even got there,' suggested Ajit.

'Unless one of us *is* a spy?' said Kim.

CHAPTER 30

Joe refused to believe that any of his classmates could be spying for someone who wanted to steal the secrets of Atlantis. But all the way back to Hillsborough he sneaked glances at each of them in turn, just checking if they looked in any way worried or shifty. He caught Kim doing the same thing and they exchanged a thin smile.

They met up with Mokie at a small guest house outside the town, where he had brought along a big holdall full of their changes of clothes. Dinner was already waiting for them.

'Excellent, I'm starved,' said Craig. 'What is it?'

'It's a local delicacy, called pepperpot, with potatoes and callaloo,' replied Mokie.

'It looks like stew, with spuds and cabbage,' said Joe.

'Well, I suppose it is,' said Mokie, 'but this is most tasty. Give it a go.'

The kids tucked into their meal, which was a delicious meaty dish in a thick, rich gravy. Joe liked vegetables, so he asked for more callaloo, which tasted like spinach.

While they ate, Kalvin was called away, but returned almost immediately.

'OK people, I'm afraid it's time to go,' he said. 'Can you finish that in ninety seconds? We have to be back at the island as soon as possible, and I'll load the car up again while you eat.'

The five didn't bother to discuss this latest development as they were keen to cram as much of the delicious pepper-pot into their mouths as they could before they went back to the same old menu in the academy.

When Kalvin called 'time's up' they waved their thanks to the staff and bundled into the back of the SUV.

'What's up, Kalvin?' asked Kim, as their transport raced back to the harbour.

'I haven't been told,' he said. 'I was just ordered to make sure you all get back as soon as possible. Luce sounded angry.'

The news of Luce's bad mood ensured the return journey was subdued, but the five felt strangely relieved to be back 'home' on Atlantis. Luce took Kalvin and Mokie aside for a short, animated conversation before ushering the students back underground.

'Please go straight to the lecture hall,' she insisted.

The five followed her instruction and when they arrived sat in their usual chairs. They were followed into the room by Ross, the security officer, and Luce, who waited silently for a minute before they were joined by the captain.

'Good evening, and I hope you had a good day,' said Luce. 'We have completed our search and are confident we have now found the reason why the drone has been following us – which we believe it has been since we left Clew Bay.'

Ross stepped forward. 'We have found a piece of technology that acts as a beacon, sending out a signal which the drone can track. I'm sorry to say this – but the beacon was brought aboard Atlantis by one of you.'

The five students were stunned, but after a couple of seconds they began to glance sideways at one another, hoping to catch a glimpse of a guilty conscience. The adults also studied each child's expression, for the same reason.

After about ten seconds, Ross resumed speaking.

'We will interview each of you separately, in turn, to ensure we learn as much as we can about this episode. Kim and Ajit, go to your rooms. Craig, go to the canteen, and

Jess wait in the common room. Joe, please stay where you are.'

Joe remained in his seat while his classmates left, and as soon as the four had left Luce turned to him.

'Joe, we believe it was you who brought the transmitting beacon onto the island. This has put our whole project at risk, and may have put Victor's life's work and enormous investment in jeopardy. It may even have put our lives at risk. What do you have to say?'

Joe's face creased in anguish. He fought to keep back tears, but was also angry, and confused.

'I don't know what to say. I don't know anything about it,' he insisted.

'Well it was found in your kit bag, stapled into the lining under the bottom,' said Ross. 'It was impossible to find until we tracked it down using a scanning device.'

'I've never seen it anything like that,' insisted Joe. 'I've had that bag since my birthday – my gran bought it for me.'

Luce walked towards Joe, and sat in the seat next to him.

'Joe, you have to tell me everything you know about this bag. Where did your grandmother get it? Where do you keep it at home?'

Joe answered her questions and tried to think of anything else that may have helped.

'Who has been in contact with the holdall since you were invited to come to the Academy?' asked the captain.

Joe paused, and tried to recall the short period of time between meeting the football scout, Fry, and leaving for Clew Bay. Only he and his parents had touched the bag, he was sure of that.

'Mum packed it, and Dad lifted it into the boot of the taxi. That was it…'

Then he remembered something odd.

'But I fell asleep in the taxi. And I only woke up when he stopped to buy petrol and he slammed the boot. But why did he need to open the boot to buy petrol?'

Luce looked at Ross.

'… And why did he even stop at the petrol station? The taxi drivers were all given a full tank of petrol and told not to stop on the way.'

CHAPTER 31

Joe was relieved to be off the hook – he had been really worried at one stage that they were going to expel him from the academy and throw him off the island to find his own way home. Ross, Luce and the captain asked him more questions about the bag, and the trip to Clew Bay, but they were now on the warpath for the taxi driver, not Joe.

When they were finished they buzzed the other four to return to the lecture hall.

'We are now satisfied that none of you is responsible, although one of you was the unwitting bearer of the beacon. We have studied the device and now know a little more about our pursuers.

'But first, we now need to leave Carriacou – Mokie has the device, which he is going to bring back to Barbados by boat this evening, and from there he will be able to hide it on-board an oil tanker which is en route to West Africa. Hopefully by the time they discover what we have done we will be far from here.'

Kim looked quizzically at Joe. Nobody else had even been interviewed, so he must be who they were talking about, she thought.

'Where are we going?' she asked.

Luce looked at the captain, who nodded.

'We have still to pick up Deryck St Vincent,' she reminded them. 'So we have asked him to fly to the nearest airport to here, which is in Grenada. He will get a dinghy out to meet us.'

The captain smiled. 'We have to be there before dark, which means we have to take the most direct route, which means we will be sailing over an active volcano. You will be quite safe, as the waters are well charted, but do take care and hold on tight when you hear a rumble, which happens every few minutes. The locals have a great name for it too – the volcano is called "Kick 'Em Jenny".'

Luce permitted the classmates to visit the viewing room to watch the volcano as they passed. The opening at the top of the underwater mountain – the vent – was two-hundred metres below the surface so they were able to stay clear of it. They could see bubbles escape and float past the porthole, and just as they sailed past there was a rumble and the whole ocean shook for a second.

'Wow!' gasped Jess. 'That was so cool.'

'Does it ever erupt?' asked Kim.

'Every few years, I think,' replied Luce. 'It's so far underwater that it won't do much real damage – unless you're a nearby boat – but there could be a tsunami which would be dangerous for people on the nearest islands.'

'And turtles,' pointed out Jess.

Atlantis continued its journey underwater until the captain announced it would shortly be surfacing. The classmates followed Luce down the staircase to the doorway where they waited for the new coach to arrive.

'This guy is really famous,' said Ajit. 'My dad used to talk about him all the time. He won the World Cup with the West Indies I think. He used to bowl really fast.'

'I suppose he must be really tall to bowl quickly,' said Craig.

Luce smiled. 'OK, we've fully surfaced, so you can go outside for some fresh air while I welcome Mr St Vincent aboard.'

Outside, night was only minutes away and Joe marvelled

at the gorgeous sunset that lit up the horizon. Down at the shoreline Luce helped a man out of a dinghy while the boat's owner's eyes bulged as he took in the amazing sight of this island that had just sprung up out of the ocean.

Ajit rushed down towards the new arrival, offering to help carry his suitcases, but pulled up sharply as the coach stood up straight for the first time.

'His height… that's amazing….,' whispered Craig to Joe.

Jess walked down towards the group and went to shake the coach's hand.

'Welcome, Mr St Vincent, it's a pleasure to meet you,' she smiled, bending forward and looking him straight in the eye.

'I'm delighted to be here, little humming bird, but call me Deryck,' he grinned. 'Are you one of my cricket stars?'

'No…' replied Jess, 'I'm more of an athlete, but I'll try anything.'

'Well, that's good to know,' Deryck replied, 'now let's get inside before that sun drops away under the sea.'

CHAPTER 32

Over the next few days the new coach, a jolly little man, became a great favourite with the five. Only Ajit and Joe knew how to play cricket so he had to explain it to all the rest, but he made their classes fun and they learned quickly. He could be serious when he wanted to, and Ajit made great strides at the game.

They continued their classes in maths, English and the other subjects, as well as football, rugby, tennis and athletics, the 'focus sports', as Luce called them. Joe noticed huge improvements in not just his own efforts at football, but also with the rest of the group.

'I think I might become a footballer,' said Jess over breakfast one morning. 'It's such a great feeling to score a goal.'

'Well, not everyone gets a chance to score a goal every game,' smiled Joe. 'My job back home is in defence so I have to stop people scoring. They'd never let me even go into the other team's half of the field!'

'That must be really boring,' replied Jess. 'Scoring goals is the *only* thing I want to do when I'm playing football.'

Joe chuckled. 'That's not a bad attitude I suppose, as the most valuable players are usually those who can score the most. But I'd prefer to be a midfielder, directing the team and playing a part in attack and defence. The Professor says he wants to see me playing there.'

'We're doing a lot more football than anything else at the moment,' sighed Kim. 'I do like it, but I wonder when we're going to get a chance to play rugby.'

Luce had been queueing for her food behind them, but when she was ready she sat down beside Kim and addressed the group.

'Well… apologies for listening in, but I was going to talk to you about this later,' she started. 'We're actually going to pretty much concentrate on football for the next four weeks.'

'Why?' asked Kim. 'I thought we were focusing on a number of sports this term?'

'You're right,' Luce replied, 'but we have been in touch with Victor and he has given us new instructions. You know Victor is an extremely wealthy man whose vision for a sports academy in an underwater island is what has brought us all together.

'Well, when Victor set off on the path to building Atlantis he wasn't alone. His twin brother, Aston, had come to work for him and he was put in charge of managing the Academy in the early years.

'Aston was lazy, however, and wanted results quickly. Instead of working long-term on nutrition and conditioning to develop young physiques as we do here, he looked for short-cuts, and that proved disastrous.

'Some of our students found themselves with stress injuries that should never have been allowed to develop, others lost too much weight too quickly, which can be very dangerous. But his greatest sin was to seek out chemical ways of making the children run faster or find extra strength and power. Illegal ways. As soon as Victor found out, he was sacked on the spot and banished from Atlantis.

'Unfortunately, before he left he managed to steal the blueprint – Victor's whole plan for the island and the academy. Since then he has teamed up with a man called Kratos, who owns one of the world's biggest sports equipment companies and the pair have built their own sports academy.

'Victor and Aston made contact again last year and began

to patch up their relationship – they are brothers after all and both are getting old. Aston told him about his sports academy and boasted about all the successes he has had.

'Victor grew angry at this and challenged him to a contest to see whose methods are best. Aston laughed at him and said he would only agree if Victor would put up Atlantis as a stake against his island, which he calls Hy-Brasil.

'So… what does that mean for us?' asked Joe.

'It means that we will spend the next four weeks turning you into the best footballers we can make you. Because if you aren't, and you don't win your next match, we will lose a lot more than just a trophy.

'What will we lose?' asked Ajit.

'The Academy … everything …' frowned Luce. 'Victor has decided to bet Atlantis on your next game of football.'

CHAPTER 33

Joe looked at Kim, Jess looked at Ajit, and Craig looked at the floor.

'You're not serious?' asked Kim.

'Most of us are beginners at football, and only Joe has ever played seriously before,' said Ajit.

'And I'm rubbish. That's why you picked me,' said Joe.

'Two old guys hammered us in the only match we've ever played,' said Jess.

Luce put up her hands to silence them.

'I know, I know, and I understand your concern. No one will blame you if you lose, and we lose Atlantis. But no one has given up on you – in fact Professor Kossuth has been chuckling about the challenge and reckons he can turn you into world beaters in the four weeks we have.'

'World beaters?' laughed Craig. 'That's nonsense. When are we stopping next?' he asked, 'because I just want to go home.'

Luce stared at Craig. From the way she speared a chunk

of melon, it was clear she wasn't happy.

'You won't be going home, not for four long years,' she started. 'That is in the contract your parents signed on your behalf. In return you are provided with a top-class education and top-class coaching and free food and accommodation for four years.

'After you leave here you will all be able to benefit from our graduate programme, which will look after all your educational needs as well as fitness and medical assistance if needed.

'So, let us be clear – don't for a moment think we will just let our huge investment in your future just walk out the door. You are staying – all of you,' she finished, staring them each in the eye in turn.

And with that she stood up, took her tray, and left the room.

The five were stunned, and nothing was said for almost a minute.

'Does that mean we're, like, prisoners here?' asked Jess to no one in particular.

'More like slaves,' snarled Craig.

Joe and Kim exchanged a glance.

'That's not really what this is like, Craig,' started Joe. 'This is a great opportunity for us – I for one have no plans to go back to playing left-back with Woodstock Wanderers and training in the rain before going home to do my homework and watch dancing talent shows on telly.'

'Yes,' agreed Kim. 'This place is boring at times, and they work us very hard, but you have to realise it is an amazing chance for us all.'

Ajit smiled weakly. 'What have we got to lose anyway. We can't just give up on Victor, and Luce, and Kalvin. We have to go out and play for them, and for Angela, and Fry, and Ross, everyone else who works here.'

Craig shrugged his shoulders. 'I suppose so. But it's messed up. There's no way we should be the ones with all this pressure on our heads. Just because Victor got into a stupid bet.'

Kim nodded. 'You're right, Craig, but now we will have to step up and learn as much as we can. If there's anyone here who can teach us what we need to learn, and come up with a plan, it's Professor Kossuth.'

There was a real spring in the Professor's step when he

entered the classroom. He had a wide smile on his face and was carrying a net bag full of footballs.

'Good morning, everybody, and I must say I am relishing this opportunity now our minds have been focused on this big game in the near future.'

He smiled and took a bundle of papers out of his briefcase.

'I have been studying your numbers and performance statistics and have found much of interest which may explain why you were first selected for Atlantis Academy. For example, Ajit, what is your birthday?

'January the 5th,' he replied.

'Joe?'

'January 8th.'

'Kim?

'January 19th.'

Jess revealed that her birthday was February 10th, while Craig was born on March 7th.

'Why do you think all your birthdays occur in the first ten weeks of the year you were all born?' asked the Professor.

The children all looked puzzled.

Professor Kossuth explained. 'Because almost all youth

sport is organised on the basis of age, kids born in January and those born in December are all thrown in together. But the January child is almost a year older, which means they are generally bigger, faster, and have greater motor skills.

'Some studies in Norway have shown that fifty per cent of sport stars are born between January and March, and another thirty per cent between April and June. So, kids born in the first half of the year are four times more likely to succeed at sport than the late summer and autumn-born children.

'But why is this? I suppose if you are bigger and faster than your team-mates you will stand out, and therefore get more chances to shine, and be given chances to play at a higher level or be picked out for extra training. Which of course, just makes things worse for the smaller kids, I'm afraid.

'I'm sure Luce and her team took note of your birthdays when they were identifying who to bring on this great adventure.'

The Professor pushed a button and five springy ropes dropped down from the ceiling, each attached to a ball-sized net bag.

'Drop your football into the bag,' he directed them. 'Now, this may look like some sort of punch bag, but in fact it is what I call a "header bag". I will now demonstrate the correct technique for heading a football, and you will copy me. I don't want you to repeat this too often as I don't think that would be good for you – I will give you a sponge ball for practice – but heading is an important skill and you must learn how to do it effectively and safely.

'Firstly, the only part of the head you must use is the forehead, secondly, you must close your mouth, and thirdly, keep your eyes open at all times. These are simple instructions, but you would be surprised how many adult, professional players fail to execute all three at once. You should also brace your neck as it is important that you guard against the impact.'

The Professor spent half an hour letting the five practice with sponge balls, and then with light plastic balls, before adjusting the header bags so they were level with each player's head. Ajit proved to have surprisingly strong neck muscles and was also most accurate with hitting with his forehead. The Professor then adjusted the height so each had to jump a little to head the ball.

The exercise was a lot less boring than Joe expected, and he enjoyed placing the ball with his head. He confessed to the group that in the seven games he had played that season he had only headed the ball once, because he was so wary of hurting himself.

After a short time the Professor called them to stop heading the ball, and played them a video of some of the great players scoring and defending with their head.

'Look at Cristiano Ronaldo, a very talented player on the ground but I don't think I have ever seen a better attacking header of the ball,' Kossuth gushed. 'Watch how he leaps, and almost hangs in the air, before he spears the ball with his forehead towards the goal.'

The five admired the action, and chatted some more about great players they had seen.

'Ronaldo once said something very wise, that you all should bear in mind,' smiled the Professor. 'He was asked what it took to be a great footballer and replied, "Talent is important – but it is not the key point."

'He went on to explain how players needed to learn the game, to understand it, to work at their talent. The other side of that, as I see it, is that players not blessed with great talent can still rise in the sport by working hard and learning from the masters. And I, you lucky children, am a master.'

CHAPTER 34

Joe really enjoyed that all the sports classes were now focused on football, and even more that the school subjects part of the Academy had been reduced to just two hours a day.

'We will have to catch up on your classes after the big game,' said Luce, 'but we will be able to bring some maths, science, geography – even history – into your learning about football.

'But today I've invited Mr St Vincent to join us, and he will talk to you about something which is one of the most important things in cricket and is also vital to a good footballer. But I'll let him explain.'

The tiny West Indian walked in and sat on the edge of the large table which stood at the top of the room. Craig and Ajit exchanged a grin as the coach's short legs dangled above the floor.

'Decisions, decisions,' he smiled. 'I suppose I had to make many thousands of them every game I ever played. Good decision-making is the key to being a good cricketer.

'As a batsman, you even need to decide how and where exactly you're going to stand. You need to make decisions based on how the bowler grips the ball, where he delivers it from, where and how high it bounces, the angle it is coming at you from, and then you must decide where you want to hit the ball, whether to defend, or attack. And many, many other factors come into it, such as where the fielders are standing, and wind, and distance to the rope. And then you must decide whether to run or not, and how many times too.

'*And* … you must decide all these things in less than half a second. Doubts about any of these decisions can be fatal, in cricket terms, and then you lose your wicket.

'Now, lots of these decisions are based on experience, on years of preparing for that moment so your instinct takes over and you know just what to do without having to think about it.

'It's the same in football, although I admit I was never very good at that. I did, however, once dribble the ball between a very tall central defender's legs,' he chuckled.

'To get better at football you must be aware of the decisions you have to make and how they can affect your team. Football is a simpler game than cricket and the range of options will be smaller. Imagine having the ball at your feet – Do you pass? Who do you pass to, left or right, short or long? Do you dribble past your opponent? When do you shoot?

'Entire games can swing on you making the right decision, and the very best footballers are the ones who aren't afraid to make those decisions.

'We will work on showing you when and how these key moments arise and how you should respond. It will mean a little time in here watching videos, but a lot more time outside with the Prof and a football.'

'Where are we at the moment?' asked Kim.

Luce stepped forward. 'Good question, Kim, because we are close to the coast of South America, off a country called Guyana. We will be able to surface shortly, and practise for a week or so before we head off to our final destination just down the coast.'

'And where is that?' asked Craig.

'Well, where do you expect the most important football match in the history of Atlantis to be played? We're heading for the home of football, the greatest soccer nation in the world ...'

CHAPTER 35

The sun was high in the sky when Atlantis surfaced, and the glare was so strong it might have blinded the children had Luce not handed them each a pair of wraparound shades. The glasses had an elasticated strap to stop them from falling off, which was just as well as Joe kept falling over.

'Sorry, Professor,' he smiled, 'I think I need a longer stud on my boots. The ground is a bit softer than usual.' He squatted down and pushed his thumb into the artificial turf.

Kalvin frowned and consulted his control box. 'Hmmm. I think you're right – but I can adjust that,' he said.

Joe noticed his thumb was being pushed back up as the ground dried out almost instantly. He never ceased to marvel at the wonders of Atlantis.

'Look at that,' gurgled Ajit, pointing to a large sea bird which was soaring back and forth across the island, before settling on top of the high fence that prevented footballs splashing into the sea.

'That's a Brown Booby,' said Jess, before suddenly blushing. 'I know, I know, I'm a bit of a nerd about birds, especially sea birds. They're related to gannets that we see back home.'

'That's very interesting,' said the Professor, 'now let's get back to business and welcome your new football coaches.'

The football master was joined by Katrina, who had been teaching them track and field, and Deryck St Vincent. Fry, the scout who had first invited Joe, had also joined the coaching staff.

The Professor began speaking. 'Right, what will happen now – and every morning before the game – is that each of you will spend one hour with each of us, one-to-one, learning movement and other skills specific to football. Each of the coaches has been briefed on your particular talent and what you need to work on to turn you into excellent footballers. The rest of the morning, and all afternoon, will be spent on game play, with a one-hour wind down indoors at which we will review what we learned.

'Any questions,' he asked.

'Yes, I have one,' piped up Craig. 'There are four coaches – but there's five of us?'

'Ah, I'm sorry,' said the Professor. 'There is one other person on the staff of the Sports Academy that was a top-class footballer – he even played in the Champions League for his club before injury ended his career. He has been here since Atlantis was built and I assure you he knows more about the art of goalkeeping than anyone I have ever met.

'Craig, you will be working with Kalvin.'

Craig opened his mouth, but no words came out.

The giant handyman stepped forward, held out his hands, palms forward, and roared laughing. 'These are the hands that stopped Bayern Munich for ninety minutes, and Manchester United too. I will do my best to make sure you stop everything Hy-Brasil can throw at you.'

Each of the adults took one of the children to a different corner of the field, while Kalvin and Craig headed for the goal areas.

It was hard work for the kids, especially those who had never had any previous soccer coaching, but they all learned fast and the Professor was delighted with their progress, as he told them at the review session at the end of the afternoon.

'You are all going to be good footballers. Perhaps one or

two of you could become very good footballers indeed. But if you all work as hard and learn as quickly as you all did today, then I think Kratos' and Aston's team will be waving the white flag of surrender by half-time.'

With no homework to be done, Luce gave them the evening off and organised a screening of the latest Hollywood block-buster in the Atlantis cinema. As he munched popcorn, Joe looked around at his team-mates – Jess was already asleep, and Ajit looked as if he was about to lose the battle with his eyelids to remain open. Craig was concentrating hard on the movie, and repeated every punch thrown by the heroes. Kim seemed to be enjoying it too, although she was laughing at all the bits that weren't supposed to be funny.

'Are we meant to take this seriously?' she sniggered at Joe, who was sitting beside her.

'I don't know, I'm finding it hard to concentrate,' he admitted.

'Look at those guys in their leotards – which police or army in the world wears leotards to fight its enemies? So why does every superhero feel the need to wear something that makes you feel like you're wearing hardly anything?'

Joe shrugged. 'I don't think too hard about this stuff, to be honest. It's just something to watch when we're relaxing.'

'Well, I don't feel too relaxed,' said Kim. 'I'm just bored. Want to go for a walk?'

'Where?' said Joe, 'we can't get outside, and I've been down every corridor two hundred times by now.'

'Follow me, I've an idea,' replied Kim, leading the way out of the tiny cinema.

She led Joe down to the practice room and switched on the control panel. Two walking machines sprang up out of compartments buried in the floor.

'OK, now, you have to use your imagination a bit, but if I switch on some of the golf course simulators…'

She tapped a command into the computer and the walls suddenly turned from plain white to a blaze of green.

'We're now here in Augusta National, you know, where they play the Masters. It's a gorgeous course and we can have a very nice walk looking at the lovely scenery,' she grinned.

Joe laughed. 'So, we get a night off, and your idea of fun is to get back on the exercise machines and study a golf course.

I can see why everyone thinks you're going to be the biggest star of us all.'

Kim frowned. 'Do people say that? Honestly, I just wanted a change of scenery. We can switch off the exercise machines, I thought that would just make it seem more like we were going for a walk.'

'No, no,' said Joe, 'let's take a stroll around Augusta. Now, show me this place they call the Amen Corner.'

CHAPTER 36

The team spent a week practising above ground before Luce told them, one breakfast time, that they needed to move Atlantis once more.

'We'll be leaving as soon as the sun starts to set, so get a full day's training in because we will be unlikely to be able to surface tomorrow.'

The Professor decided to replay the first game the kids had ever played together – against himself and Kalvin. This time it was a very different story, and result. The five were much more in tune with their teammates, and their skill level had risen so that they were able to pass much more accurately and Jess had turned into a very accurate shooter. Only once did one of her shots rocket away wide and rattle the back fence, disturbing the slumber of the Brown Booby, who had seemed to have made his home on Atlantis.

Kalvin was still very hard to beat in goal, but Jess was able to score twice and with Craig in brilliant form at the other end the game ended in a deserved draw.

'Now that was a fantastic game, and a heartening improvement by each and every one of you,' the Professor smiled.

The kids trekked uphill into the cottage, kicking their footballs in front of them. Jess stopped to wave goodbye to the sea bird, who she had named Brian and now regarded as a lucky mascot.

'I wonder where he'll go now?' she asked.

'Well, unless he's got a snorkel he wouldn't want to hang around on top of that fence,' chuckled Ajit.

'He'd better shoo right now,' said Kalvin, 'I've got to slide the fence back underground to get ready for diving,' clicking a button on the console which made the goalposts withdraw.

'Can we go upstairs to the viewing room to watch the submerging?' asked Joe. 'I'd love to see what it looks like.'

Luce looked at Kalvin. 'All right, if Kalvin agrees to bring you, and you all agree to stay in the room and sit down and hold tight at all times, then you can go up there. See you downstairs for dinner afterwards.'

After Kalvin had finished ensuring the overground part of the island was ready to submerge, he led the children to the viewing room on the top deck. They settled in and awaited the signal from the captain. Joe gazed out the window as the sun started to sink below the horizon, and the engines driving Atlantis rumbled into life.

'Action stations, ready to dive,' came the call over the loudspeaker.

As the island gradually dropped beneath the waves, the children marvelled as the sunset rose higher in the sky as they looked out.

'There's Brian,' gasped Jess, as the sea bird flew across the windows, twisting his head as he passed.

'Yuck, his eyes are bright red,' said Craig. 'Is that natural?'

'I don't know,' frowned Jess, 'maybe it's just the weird sunset?'

'Let's not worry about that now,' said Kalvin, 'hold tight, we're about to go under…'

And with that the island dropped underwater, with nothing left on the surface to show they had ever been there except a few scattered brown feathers.

CHAPTER 37

The children spent the next day working with the Professor on formation drills, planning for who would slip into position should one player be taken out of the game for a short time while play carried on. He also suggested some changes to their attacking formation, but left Joe to decide where and when they would be used.

'Remember, I will not be out on the field with you. You will hear me shouting instructions occasionally, but I am not very keen on coaches who try to run the game from the sideline. I prefer to give you all the information and skills you require, and then to let you make your own decisions as players out on the pitch.

'Our training has come together very well, and I am confident that you will be able to withstand most opponents. Certainly, any side Hy-Brasil can put out at this short notice.'

Luce called down to see them at dinner, and after slipping them an extra treat for afters, she capped it all by telling them that this evening they would be allowed have a video conference with their families.

It had been so long since Joe had seen his parents that he wondered did he look any different. There were no barbers or hairdressers on Atlantis, so his hair was starting to grow past the collar when he wore a polo shirt. Maybe he'd let it grow like one of those French players.

The kids were asked not to talk about where they were now sailing, or where they had been at all on the voyage, and definitely not to tell their parents that Victor had just put up the whole island for a bet with his twin brother.

'You look skinny,' said Joe's mother. 'Are they feeding you at all?'

'We're getting loads of food, really nice food,' insisted Joe. 'But we're doing an awful lot of running around too. Honestly, I feel great.'

'I hope all that running around isn't affecting your studies,' said his father.

'Well ... we've been doing a bit less for the last few weeks,' admitted Joe, 'but honestly, we were doing plenty of school work. I've learnt a lot more than I would have at home – there's only five of us in the class.'

His dad was also keen to find out about where he was, but Joe said they'd been sworn to secrecy. They didn't even know he was on an underwater island, which was probably just as well.

His parents filled him in on the news from home, and how Woodstock Wanderers had been doing – not very well – but there was talk that a scout from Arsenal had been over to check Robbie out.

Talk of Wanderers suddenly made Joe very homesick, and a lump started to form in his throat. He tried to hurry the conversation to a close.

'They're calling us for dinner now,' he lied. 'You know how important regular meals are, Mam.'

They said their goodbyes, and Joe felt a tear escaping as his mother started to cry on the other end of the link.

'I'll see you soon enough,' he called, but Kalvin had already cut the connection.

'I saw you were struggling there, Joe,' he smiled. 'But everyone gets like that.'

He mentioned the most famous rugby player in the world, a tough forward who would-be tacklers bounced off.

'I remember when he was here – he cried every single

night. It's completely normal.'

Joe swallowed the lump and wiped his eyes. 'Thanks, Kalv. I don't miss home usually, but seeing them there, and Mam's red eyes…' he trailed away.

'Red eyes,' he gasped.

'Kalvin, can you bring me to Luce? Right now – it's really urgent.'

CHAPTER 38

The manager's eyes widened as Joe explained what he had seen and his theory about what it might mean.

'Right, stay there, I'll go see the captain.'

Luce raced off to the bridge while Kalvin and Joe shrugged their shoulders.

'That's an amazing idea, Joe,' said the giant handyman, 'you think he could have been spying on us all week?'

'I suppose so. He was always there. We have to get back up there to check.'

Luce returned and told them they would be resurfacing immediately. She told Kalvin to take Joe and his classmates back to the viewing room and remain there until she came for them.

Back in the room Joe remained silent as the rest of his team joined him. Jess rushed to portholes as soon as they surfaced, but she complained that she couldn't see Brian the Brown Booby.

Joe squinted his eyes to focus on the distance and could distinctly see a cluster of red lights in the same part of the sky as he had seen the drone weeks before. As soon as the island re-emerged from the water the lights seemed to grow brighter, and slightly bigger.

'I think it's coming closer,' whispered Kalvin to Joe.

Joe looked down at the ocean and was startled to see that a dinghy with an outboard engine had cast off from Atlantis and was making speed towards the lights.

The rest of the team spotted it too and watched as the two men race across the waves in the little orange boat.

'Can we use the binoculars?' asked Ajit, as he took a pair down from a rack on the wall. Kalvin nodded and six pairs of eyes zoomed in on the tiny craft, although Jess soon became distracted and scanned the skies.

'There's Brian – or one of his family anyway,' she smiled. 'His eyes are still a bit bright though.'

The men had travelled more than a kilometre from the island when they suddenly stopped. One man lifted something from the bottom of the dinghy and passed it to the other man who removed it from its case.

'He's got a rifle!' called Craig. 'What's he going to shoot

out there – there's nothing to be seen?'

Joe winced as Jess realised what was about to happen.

'No! He's going to shoot Brian!' she cried.

'That's not Brian,' Joe said, resting his hand on Jess's arm.

A single shot rang out and all eyes switched to where it had been aimed.

All they could see was something small and dark drop straight down, with a trail of feathers coming behind.

Jess wailed, insisting that her favourite sea bird – or one like him – had just been shot.

'That's *so* against the law,' she said. 'I'm going to report Luce to … to … to whoever's the nearest police.'

The children watched the sailors rush across to collect the remains of their target and ferry it back to Atlantis.

'What just happened there?' asked Kim. 'You seem to know more than you're telling us, Joe.'

Joe shrugged his shoulders once again. 'Sorry, Kim, Luce told me not to say – she'll be back in a minute.'

'Why did they shoot Brian?' wailed Jess. 'Was that your idea?'

It took ten minutes for Luce to return to the viewing room.

'I'm sorry about the delay, but we had to make the device safe,' she explained.

'What device?' demanded Kim. 'That was a *bird* they just shot!'

'No,' said Luce, glancing across at Joe and grateful that he had kept quiet. 'It wasn't a bird. Joe noticed the bird had red eyes that reminded him of the drone that had been following us – and we thought it important to check it out.

'Our sailors checked it on their scanners when they were out there and they discovered it was made of metal, which is why they shot it out of the sky. They collected the debris and it was indeed a drone carrying a very, very clever device which is likely to have been transmitting video from your training sessions.

'We presume Kratos is behind this and the captain is currently on the phone to Victor explaining the situation. If they know all your plans and tactics I'm sure he'll want to cancel the bet and call off the game.'

Joe felt his heart sink. After all the work they had put in preparing for the game, it would be very disappointing not to play it. He noticed the others looking at him with long faces too.

'Hey, don't blame me,' he said. 'I only saved us from those spies. It could have been dangerous.'

'I know,' grumped Craig, 'it's just if you kept your mouth shut we'd still be going somewhere amazing to play football. Now… who knows?'

CHAPTER 39

Atlantis remained above water, and although Professor Kossuth insisted that they join him for training next morning, the children's hearts weren't in it.

As they stopped for a water break, a sound began to break the silence of the morning.

Whuppa, whuppa, whuppa – the kids scanned the sea and the skies to see what was causing it. The sound grew louder and the tiny speck on the horizon grew bigger until they realised that a helicopter was its way to Atlantis.

'Return to the cottage,' insisted the Professor, 'and leave me to see what this aircraft brings to us.'

Kim and Joe stood at the window and watched as the helicopter came in to land in the middle of the football pitch.

The Professor stepped out towards it as the side door opened, and out stepped an elderly gentleman who looked a little familiar. Kalvin opened the door to the cottage and ushered the youngsters outside.

'Ah, so this is my Atlantis United team,' smiled the newcomer, who was well groomed and wore an expensive blue suit and purple silk tie. 'We meet again.'

'And who are you?' asked Craig. 'I don't think we've met?'

The old man adopted a funny pirate accent. 'Arrrr, Oi'm the cap'n of the good ship *Pirate Queen*,' he chuckled, and all five of the kids' eyes widened together.

'You're King Victor,' laughed Jess. 'And that's a much nicer way to come on board than that old ship you had for us. Why couldn't we have a trip in a helicopter!'

Victor joined in the laughter.

'Well, I apologise for that, but there were security issues which forced us to act as we did – as I'm sure you now understand,' he added, before looking at Joe and smiling.

'Now, let me go inside for a quick chat with Luce and the captain, and then I'll come out and see how you are getting on with your football training. Maybe we could have one of those famous 5 versus 2 games that the Professor and Kalvin are so fond of organising for their own entertainment.'

The visit of the island's owner seemed to energise the children, and they threw themselves into the rest of the training session with new spark.

'So, these five against two games are a regular thing,' said

Kim to Joe, as they waited for Ajit to put his right boot back on after it flew off in a tackle.

'I wonder how many of the previous kids' team even got a draw or scored a goal?' said Joe.

'Well, I'd say that guy in the hallway must have scored a few,' laughed Kim, referring to the star striker from Chile who had won the golden boot in Europe in each of the last three seasons.

'Actually, he only scored once against us in his four years,' smiled the Professor, who had been listening in. 'Although Kalvin and I are a few years older now…'

CHAPTER 40

When his meeting was over Victor came outside and offered to referee the game between the kids and their two coaches.

Both sides took it very seriously, with Kalvin unbeatable in the first half. Craig had also been excellent, saving the only two shots the Professor was allowed get off.

So with the score at nil-nil, Victor blew the whistle to start the second half. 'Just ten minutes this half,' he announced. 'It's too hot to referee so it must be too hot to play.'

Joe was enjoying the battle in midfield with Professor Kossuth, and he had the better of him on a few occasions. The older man was able to do almost magical things with the football, which sometimes seemed to Joe as if it was attracted to his boot by an extra strong magnet.

'Give him the sandwich treatment,' whispered Victor as Joe trotted past in pursuit of the Professor. 'If you both tackle him at once he won't be able to do his tricks.'

Joe told Ajit his plan and next time Professor Kossuth

got the ball they both closed in on him. Ajit ran alongside his left shoulder and angled his own across to meet it. The Prof flicked the ball to avoid Ajit's lunge, but Joe nipped in and stole it right off his toe. Joe pushed the ball ahead of him and with one bound he was out of the coach's range. He looked up and saw Jess on the edge of the area, but racing towards him. As he drew Kalvin out towards him, he speared a pass with the outside of his boot which just beat the goalkeeper's left hand, leaving Jess to sidefoot the ball into an empty net.

'Yippee!' screamed Jess as she leapt in the air and the rest of Atlantis United rushed to congratulate her. The Professor looked ashen-faced and tried to avoid the gaze of Victor as he pointed to the centre spot.

'How long is left, referee?' asked Kim.

'Ninety seconds or so,' replied Victor.

Joe decided that defence was the best option for his Atlantis side so he urged all his team to retreat behind the ball, but that also meant that Kalvin was able to join The Professor for the kick-off. It was all or nothing now for the senior side.

For a big, lumbering man, Kalvin was remarkably fast

on his feet, but Kim marked him closely and the Professor grew impatient at not being able to find any space. Joe and Ajit never let him get past them, while Jess hovered around the edge of the Atlantis penalty area ready to lend a hand where she was needed.

The Professor's mind was whirring fast, they all could see that, but no-one was sure where he would make his move. He looked up at the goal, and from just ten metres inside the opposition's half, he lifted his leg back as far as it would go and swung down quickly. He had calculated the power, distance and wind speed in his head, and reckoned the ball would fly into the top left hand of the goal about six centi-metres under the crossbar and another six from the upright.

The ball flew high into the air, almost like a rugby kick, and dipped as it began returning to earth. Joe looked on with horror as he watched Craig try to work out the angle at which the ball was coming towards the goal.

'Jump! Now!' called Joe, as the keeper continued to dither.

Craig took two steps across the goal-line and leapt as high in the air as he could. He stretched his arm out as long as he could make it and flicked his extra-large style keepers' gloves at the descending ball. His fingertips brushed against it, but that was just enough and the ball was deflected off target, bounced off the goalpost to Kim who controlled it and ran away upfield with Kalvin chasing after her.

Kim was about to fire the ball into the empty net when a loud whistle sounded two blasts and Victor raised his arm straight in the air over his head.

'That's it, game over,' he called.

'Ah, ref,' complained Joe. 'She was sure to score.'

'Now, now,' chuckled Victor. 'You don't want to go too hard on the elderly gentlemen, do you?'

The Atlantis team were still overjoyed by their result and were given great cheers from the crew of the submarine island who had heard the scoreline and rushed to see the historic first defeat for the football coaches.

'Well, that was a very entertaining game,' announced Victor. 'And a wonderful result. In all the years of our Academy the staff have always beaten – and usually hammered – the pupils. So I see this result as a win for both sides – there is no way your team would have won the game without Professor Kossuth's brilliant coaching, which of course is the main reason he works here.

'However, it does set a bad example, and if it ever happens again I'm afraid I will have to sack the Professor and Kalvin,' he added with a grin, winking at the beaten side.

CHAPTER 41

Victor joined his five students for dinner, and he was full of questions about how they were getting on at Atlantis Academy.

'But you must have some questions for me too,' he said as they finished up their main course. 'I'll be happy to answer any of your questions, except about this game against Hy-Brasil because Ross has yet to finish his investigation and Luce and I will need to have a serious discussion about what it all means.'

Kim asked Victor why he had built Atlantis.

'Because I wanted you, and dozens of other children just like you, to have the best chance of fulfilling your sporting dreams by becoming as good as you can be.

'When I was your age I was a very ordinary player of football, tennis, hurling, rugby, and many other sports. But I loved sport – every sport – and threw myself passionately into it as soon as I discovered a new one.

'But I was never able to improve because there weren't

nearly enough coaches and the ones we did have only concentrated on the really excellent players. I became convinced that there was a fantastic footballer inside me if I could only find a coach to believe in me and bring that great player out.

'But it never happened, and that made me sad. So when I became successful in my life, earning greater wealth than I ever could spend, I decided to try to give other children the chance I never had. I then set up a network of coaches and scouts to go out and look at underage football teams – not to identify the best players, but the find the weakest. Then I had people investigate how passionate those children were about their pursuit – I wanted kids who lived every spare moment for their sport – whether they were the type of kid who practised on their own, for example,' he added.

Angela came in with a tray of drinks and some of Victor's favourite chocolate biscuits as treat. Victor stirred his cup of green tea and opened the wrapper on a small bar. He took one bite before he laid it down and carried on with his story.

'We looked at tens of thousands of eleven-year-olds and whittled it down to about a dozen before we invited them to join our football camp. Some of their parents were unsure, but the kids saw the opportunity we gave them with the best coaches and facilities laid on. The camp just lasted for eight weeks in summer, based deep in a forest in Scotland, but two of that first group improved so much that they played underage international football before they were fifteen. One later became a professional with a lower-league team in England.

'But the summer camp was very limiting. I wanted to expand our range to far more sports, but also to restrict the numbers we recruited to just a handful of pupils. We developed plans for an island off the coast of England, but we found that sports clubs started spying on us and trying to steal our methods or poach our players before we were finished developing them.

'Then we looked at buying and converting an aircraft-carrier into a floating school which could visit lots of countries and sample the different sports and sporting cultures around the world – but that would have been too easy for spies to track as we travelled around the seas.

'So…' he smiled, 'I woke up in the middle of the night with this mad idea to build an island that could move around the oceans, which meant we could visit all those places, but also submerge like a submarine when you wanted to stay out of sight and work in privacy.

'And that's where we are!' he announced, with a flourish of his arms.

'It must have cost you millions,' said Ajit.

'Hundreds of millions, I'd say,' replied Victor, 'and about a million a month to keep it afloat too. But it's my pride and joy. And when I leave this world I know I'll have helped hundreds of young people to improve and enrich their lives in an important way.'

Kalvin popped his head around the canteen door and signalled to Victor.

'I'd best follow Prince Kalvin,' he joked. 'But I will talk to you later – as soon as we decide what is happening. However, after watching you today, I am confident you can beat anyone they can throw at us.'

CHAPTER 42

'I hope we get the chance to play this High Brazil crowd,' said Jess. 'It would be such a waste of an amazing place to let them just steal it away from us.'

'I agree,' said Kim. 'This has been Victor's life's work. If we do get a chance to play for it we must remember that. We have to do our very best.'

'Obviously,' sniffed Craig. 'I just think it's really unfair that it falls on our shoulders.'

The five cleaned their plates away and were so exhausted after their efforts in the match that after they returned to their rooms they all went straight to bed.

Joe lay outside the duvet reading a book – his body might have been tired, but his brain needed something more to get him to sleep. He loved reading, especially about sport, and he enjoyed putting himself inside the mind of the hero. This book's main character was a hopeless rugby player at first, but met the ghost of an old player who gave him hints on how to get better and it seemed to work.

Joe closed the book and smiled. He knew he wasn't much use when he played with Woodstock Wanderers, but he knew he had improved and he was one of the stars of his new team. He was pretty sure Kalvin and the Prof weren't ghosts too.

When they returned to the canteen next morning for breakfast, Luce and Victor were already tucking into bowls of muesli and banana.

Joe, Craig and Ajit sat down at the next table and said hello.

'Good morning,' said Victor. 'We'd better wait for Kimberley and Jessica to arrive before we start.'

'I don't think her name is Kimberley,' laughed Ajit. 'Her mum and dad are Chinese and Kim is a common enough name over there. It's just Kim.'

Victor laughed, and at that moment Kim and Jess walked in. Victor explained his error, and Kim smiled at his apology.

'But enough of Victor's stupidity,' chipped in Luce. 'He has something very important to tell you.'

The five sat forward and stared at the old man as he stirred his tea.

'Well, you know already that we discovered the "sea bird" was actually a drone that was being used to track our island. Our investigations have found even more alarming details – that the bird's eyes acted as a video camera, recording everything it saw and transmitting it back to whoever controlled it.'

'But it was sitting up on top of the fence all week!' gasped Ajit.

'And it was spying on all our plans,' sighed Jess.

'But who would have done that,' asked Craig. 'Your brother?'

'Perhaps,' replied Victor, 'but he has denied it, and I have to believe him. I know him better than anyone and I think I know when he is lying. He has changed, and we want to be friends again.'

'Who else would have done it though?' asked Joe.

'We are still investigating,' replied Luce.

'We are very upset and concerned at what we have discovered, but on the balance of things, we have to go ahead with the game. I gave Aston my word about what would be at stake, and he has given me his that Hy-Brasil is not behind the spying. There are other rivals in my world, people who wish to steal our secrets, so we will continue to search for answers. But right now, with nine days to go, I want you to concentrate on getting tuned up for this game.'

CHAPTER 43

The five young footballers worked very hard in the training rooms. Atlantis had a gym, but the strength and conditioning coach, Connor, wouldn't let them near any of the equipment that they had seen used on television.

'Your bodies haven't grown enough to use weights or these machines. That will come, but don't rush it. There's plenty of other things we can do such as push-ups, squats and resistance bands.'

Joe found the gym boring, but made up little number games in his head to help him get through it. Craig loved it, however, and revelled in being the best at most of the exercises they did.

'Is there any exercise you can do to make you taller?' he asked Connor.

The rest of the kids laughed, but the coach just smiled and nodded.

'Actually there are a few theories on that,' he said. 'The only ones I agree with are swimming and stretching. I'll give you a few you can do on your own – but everyone should make sure they get twenty minutes swimming in every day, as its good for lots of things.'

Professor Kossuth was concerned that his plans for the game had been leaked to their opponents, and he set about working on some alternatives.

'Do not abandon our first plans though,' he told them. 'It will become obvious if Hy-Brasil are aware of our tactics or not, so look on these as Plan B, or even Plan C. It is always good to have a few different approaches if your opponent is not as you expected.'

'What do you expect them to be like?' asked Joe.

'I expect them to bigger and stronger than you,' said the Professor. 'They usually recruit players from the USA and Canada, where children are on average taller and heavier at every age band. But there's nothing we can do about that at this stage. You must strive to beat them by being faster, more skilful, and quicker thinking.'

'When do we arrive at where we play them?'

'We've already arrived,' said the Professor.

'You mean we're playing them here on the island?' asked

Kim.

'Yes, and obviously after we surface. But no, we're actually in the exact spot where Victor and Aston have agreed to play the game.'

'And where is that?' asked Jess.

'I can't say, but you will find out soon enough. I've just had a message to say we will be surfacing in fifteen minutes. And I've been told to tell you to go to the canteen and await instructions.'

The kids tucked into a small meal while they waited to be told to strap in for surfacing. They were all nervous, but most kept silent and left Jess to bubble away, coming up with increasingly wacky suggestions for where they might be.

'It could be the North Pole?' she speculated.

'Two days sail away from Guyana – on the equator?' Ajit pointed out.

'Maybe they can go quicker than we thought?'

'No, it's not going to be the North Pole,' said Kim. 'Remember, Luce said we were going just down the coast.'

Joe wished he had remembered his world geography

classes.

'I had a look in the atlas after she said that, and I think I know where we are going. Well, roughly anyway.'

'Where?' demanded Jess.

'I won't say, but if I'm right then it's a very fitting place for an epic football match.'

CHAPTER 44

The five were summoned to the cottage where Victor and Luce were waiting. Kalvin opened the doors and they trekked out onto the island.

The first thing Joe noticed was how hot it had suddenly become, and how hard it was to breathe. The island had surfaced in the middle of a very wide river, surrounded on both banks by high walls of jungle.

'You will now be aware of the tremendous humidity,' said Luce. 'That is why we came here a few days early, to allow you to acclimatise. You are here in one of the most demanding environments on earth, and you will need to be careful not to fall ill. You have all been inoculated against most illnesses known to man, but here there are many things we do not yet understand, so take care. And never, never swim in the river – or even put your hand or toe in the water.'

'So, where are we?' asked Craig.

'I think that river is the Amazon,' said Jess.

Luce smiled, and nodded.

'So? Does that mean we're in Amazonistan?' asked Craig.

'No,' said Joe. 'We're in the greatest football nation in the world. We're in Brazil.'

'Wow, how do they get so good when they play in heat like this?' asked Ajit.

'Well, this is close to the equator,' explained Luce. 'It's a huge country and most people live three or four thousand kilometres further south. But it's hot there too.

'Now, Professor Kossuth will want to take you for some light training now, and explain a bit more about what you can or cannot do. But the most important rule is STAY OUT OF THE WATER.'

The kids heeded her warning, although none of them had a spare ounce of energy to waste on swimming after even ten minutes walking and jogging on the island. It got better next day however, and the day after that they were well able to perform as they had been before they reached Amazonia.

Joe had just slammed a pile-driver shot past Craig into the roof of the net when Kalvin came rushing out of the door to the cottage.

'OK, get away from the edges, please,' he announced. 'You need to come up here till we see what happens next.'

The coaches and pupils jogged up the hill to the small building. Jess asked Kalvin what was going on.

'Our friends from Hy-Brasil have arrived,' he announced, 'so hold tight.'

Atlantis was moored right in the middle of the Amazon, about a hundred hundred metres from the bank. About two hundred metres away downstream the waters began to bubble before, with a sound that began with a rumble and ended in a roar, an enormous dark shape began to surface. It was an island too, but nothing resembling the gentle curves and green fields of Atlantis.

Up it climbed, washing with it a wave of water that rushed over the playing field of Leap Island and stopped just short of the cottage. The enormous structure towered as high as the Kapok trees that flanked the great river and loomed over Atlantis, the highest point of which was less than half the height of Hy-Brasil.

'I can see why we're playing down here,' said Kim. 'You'd get dizzy looking up at it, I'd say it's even worse looking down.'

'They don't have the pitch surface technology to play outdoors on that island,' said Victor, who had come up to see the new arrival. 'But they're very keen to acquire our knowledge about grass.'

After a few minutes a cave opened in the side of Hy-Brasil, and a dinghy with a pilot and two other men emerged. They raced across to Atlantis and drove their boat straight onto the island.

'Apologies for that,' said the pilot. 'I didn't fancy wading ashore in this river.'

'Don't worry about it, I don't blame you,' said Victor, who reached his hand out to the older of the other two men.

'Aston,' he smiled, 'welcome back to Atlantis. I am so delighted to see you again.'

Aston moved closer and hugged his twin brother.

'Me too,' he replied. 'It has been too long. We will dine together this evening and catch up on old times.'

The other man coughed.

'Oh, I do apologise,' said Aston. 'This is my business partner, Kratos. His people run Hy-Brasil now as I'm close to retirement age.'

Kratos stepped forward and shook Victor's hand.

'Enchanted to meet you sir, you come from a remarkable family,' the newcomer said. 'But I'm afraid I'm here to take your island so I shan't be getting involved in pleasantries or joining you for dinner. We have come many thousands of kilometres today and our game kicks off three days from now, at five o'clock in the evening. May the best team win, but please excuse me.'

And with that he stepped back into the dinghy, followed by a sad-looking Aston.

CHAPTER 45

Back inside the Academy, the children were puzzled.

'Three days to go to the game, and they've just arrived? They'll never acclimatise in time,' said Kim.

'Unless they've been somewhere with a similar climate of course,' said Joe.

'But Kratos said they've come very far today,' said Ajit.

'I'm not sure I'd trust that man if I asked him to tell me the time,' said Kim.

With Hy-Brasil looming over the Atlantis pitch, the Professor decided to move indoors for the main sessions on tactics. 'We will continue to train outside, of course, and work on your stamina, which will be very important in this climate.'

As the clock ticked on and the game neared, there was a definite up-turn in nerves and tetchiness among the pupils. Craig became unbearable, snapping away at anyone that interrupted him doing anything at all.

'Just leave me alone, I'm trying to think,' he said to Jess after she had merely wished him 'Good morning' at breakfast.

'Now, now, please let's be civil to each other,' said Luce, who had just joined the table. 'We're all getting very tense, but there's no excuse for bad manners. We are on the same team – all of us.'

Craig didn't like being told off and looked down at his plate for the next half-minute before he stood up and left the room.

'Let him go,' said Luce, 'He needs to cool down. It's just his way of dealing with stress.'

The night before the game Luce invited the team up to her office for a small party. She laid on juices and snacks, with wine for the adults. Victor and Luce both said a few words of encouragement, but Joe found his mind wandering, checking out the photos dotted around the wall.

Victor finally asked the Professor to speak, but the coach seemed reluctant. He eventually stood in front of the group and pointed to each of the five in turn, before starting to speak.

'You five are the most amazing bunch of youngsters I've ever had the privilege of coaching. You aren't the most talented, but you've all shown great commitment and willingness to learn. And you have learned so much.

'Tomorrow you will go out and play for Atlantis United and show everyone just how good you are now. I have no doubt you are good enough to beat any other side your age in the world. So there won't be any pre-match session tomorrow, or any last-minute cramming of tactics and game plans. It's all there inside your heads, and inside your feet. I believe in you.'

And with that the Professor sat down.

There was silence for a few seconds before Luce went to her desk and opened a box she had hidden beneath it.

'Before you go off to bed, we have one small presentation to make, and I will ask Victor to do so.'

She lifted five packets wrapped in plastic onto the desk.

'Ah, yes, of course,' said Victor. 'These shirts have been specially designed for tomorrow's game. I hope you wear them with honour, and with pride.'

He motioned to Joe to come forward, and handed him his deep red shirt, with his surname, Wright, printed across the back.

'Kim Yuan,' he called, and Kim went up to collect her shirt.

The other three followed, and all spent a few seconds admiring their new kit before thanking Luce and Victor and bidding the Professor good night.

CHAPTER 46

Next morning, Joe rose early and took a quick scamper up the staircase to the viewing room. He stared out the window at the enormous rival island.

'That's just ridiculous,' he said to himself. 'TWO enormous underground islands built just because two brothers fell out. And now their whole future depends on a game of football.' He shook his head and descended to the breakfast room.

The others were eating a light meal, because Connor had told them that they would have a short, sharp burst of training and would be going back to sleep for three hours. Joe enjoyed being allowed to go for naps in the daytime, it felt like he was back in infants' school.

'Everyone get a good night's sleep?' asked the Professor.

Each of the five looked in different directions, all avoiding the coach's gaze.

'Not to worry, I didn't expect anyone to sleep their full nine hours the night before a game,' he chuckled. 'I knew a captain of Germany who never slept a wink before a World Cup semi-final. He was snoring in the dressing room before the game – but as soon as the referee blew his whistle he was wide awake and raring to go. He scored twice and won the man of the match award.'

'In that case I'll probably win the Golden Boot,' said Jess, yawning.

The Professor kept the conversation light, retelling a few funny stories from his past and avoiding the subject of the big game. At eleven o'clock he waved them all away.

'If you're still yawning at my tales you must be tired Jess – because you can't be bored by them!'

The five retired to their rooms and, sure enough, found it much easier to sleep because they were relaxed.

At two o'clock in the afternoon they awoke to the sound of a buzzer, followed by Kalvin's voice telling them to meet him outside.

The team joined their goalkeeping coach up top, and he took them on a couple of very gentle laps of the field to warm their muscles. The rest of their bodies were pretty warm too, so they all took great care to drink plenty of water.

At three o'clock they went down below for a massage, and

Joe spent some time with Fry practising penalties against a virtual reality video of the best goalkeepers in the world. He could never get more than one goal out of every five shots, but reckoned that was a pretty good strike rate.

Craig called into the room too, for the same reason. He wasn't able to stop more than one in five of Ronaldo's penalties but he was delighted that he had even got one.

They sat on the bench, watching old videos of Champions League finals.

'I just wish this would start,' complained Craig. 'I want it to be over with.'

'Me too,' said Joe, 'but I'm also looking forward to seeing what our opposition are like, and how much of a test they will be for us. It was hard playing against the two-man team, but it will be very different taking on five opponents.'

'I've been doing a few of those stretches Connor suggested,' said Craig, 'as well as a lot of swimming and doing a bit of hanging from the bars too. And – would you believe? – I've grown an extra two centimetres.'

'That's amazing,' said Joe, although he sounded a bit dubious. 'I wish I could grow a bit too, but I think I'll leave it to nature.'

At four o'clock the pair wandered back to the canteen and munched on a couple of energy bars and some fruit juice. The rest of the team joined them, all now dressed in the red of Atlantis United, and the Professor also slipped into the room.

'I promised you I wouldn't confuse your minds with last minute cramming – you all know what to do and when to do it. If anyone has any questions I'm here to answer them…'

The kids all shook their heads, or said 'no, thanks Professor.'

'OK, so there's just one thing I have left to do – and that is name the captain. Different people have shown different leadership skills these past few months. And I hope to see everyone do that out on the field today. But football demands a captain – to shake hands with his opponent on all your behalf before the game, but also to make the big calls once it has begun. And I, with Kalvin and Fry, have decided that the person with the deepest knowledge of football, and the greatest awareness of the strategies we will use, shall wear the armband today. So, we have chosen Joe.'

Joe was stunned. He supposed as the only one to play football before meant he was a sort-of obvious choice, but he had never seen himself as a leader. It was his dream to captain Woodstock one day, once he had nailed down a place on the team. Now here he was captaining Atlantis United.

CHAPTER 47

Joe led the team out the door of the cottage and was surprised to see the touchline already lined with dozens of spectators, most waving red scarves.

'Why are they wearing scarves in this heat?' asked Ajit.

'They're supporters – Atlantis supporters,' replied Kim. 'That must be everyone that works on Atlantis. There's Ross, and Maureen, Fleur and Angela from the canteen.'

The players felt a bit weird at first, having a kick-about in front of the people they saw every day, but they soon focused on their main task and went through their stretches and warm-ups with Connor.

With ten minutes to kick off, Joe glanced over at Hy-Brasil in time to see the cave door open and a small fleet of dinghies emerge. The first one had five passengers, all wearing bright yellow shirts. The pilot steered them across the short trip across to Atlantis and they clambered onto the island one by one.

'They're huge!' said Jess, as their opponents stood up and

looked around the arena.

True enough, some of the four boys and one girl in yellow shirts looked more like men and women. One even had a moustache.

Victor walked over to greet his brother, and Kratos, to the game. 'Good afternoon, and welcome to Atlantis. But I must say I'm astonished that you have brought these players – they are far older than ours.'

Aston began to reply, but Kratos butted in. 'Why of course they are, King Victor. Your students have been with you for four months, ours have been with us for four years. No one said anything about them being the same age or having spent the same amount of time in the academy.

'But…' began Victor. 'These are almost fully-grown adults.'

'Well, like I said, they have been with us for almost four years. We are about to send them out into the world. One has signed for Barcelona I believe.'

The Professor kept his face set as he listened to the conversation, but took Joe aside just before the teams lined up.

'There's nothing to worry about here, Joe, you and your team took on two adults and tore us apart by using your brains and your speed. You can do the very same here.'

The two sides took their places and the referee – who had been hired from the Brazilian FA and arrived by parachute – blew the whistle to kick-off.

The Hy-Brasil team came charging at the smaller team and tried to muscle them off the ball at every chance they got. The smallest Atlantean, Jess, hadn't a chance against the big defenders and was knocked onto the ground twice in the first five minutes. Joe spent most of his time coming back to help-out the defence, but the tackling technique he had learned from Professor Kossuth meant nothing got past him.

The yellow team grew impatient at the youngsters' refusal to crack and next time Joe got the ball he was floored by a savage tackle from behind.

He waited for the whistle for a free-kick, but when it didn't come he sprang up and pleaded, 'Hey ref?' The referee waved play on and the Hy-Brasil striker made the most of the chance to fire the ball into the top corner of the net.

There was a handful of Hy-Brasil supporters on the touchline, but their cheers were barely audible.

'Referee, I was tackled from behind – that's a foul,' said

Joe as he walked towards the centre circle.

The referee stared at Joe, and reached towards his pocket, producing a yellow card.

'What's that for?' Joe asked, but the referee didn't reply, just zipping his finger across his mouth to tell the youngster to keep quiet.

Joe was angry at the injustice, but he knew he had to calm down or he would soon find himself facing a red card which would spell disaster for his team. He took a return pass from Ajit and looked up to consider his options – Jess was making a run into the penalty box, and Ajit had ran out to left taking the midfielder with him. A yellow-shirted player lunged at Joe, but he skipped past the tackle and saw he was now alone running in on the keeper who had come out to narrow his angle to shoot.

But with a gorgeous chip straight out of the Professor's playbook he beat the keeper and watched as the ball landed on the goal-line and bounced into the goal.

The goalie jumped up and pointed to Jess who was collecting the ball from the net. '*Impedimento, impedimento,*' he screamed at the referee.

'What's he saying?' asked Joe.

'I think he's asking for "offside"' said Ajit – 'we had a Portuguese lad played hurling with us last year and he used to shout that all the time.'

The referee looked at Jess before waving his arms for a free-out, although he looked embarrassed to do so.

'That's a joke!' said Jess, but sensibly kept quiet when Joe warned her with a 'hush' signal with his finger over his lips.

Joe ran the 'goal' over in his head and couldn't see anything wrong with it – Jess was nowhere near the action when he shot, and the defender was nearer to the goal than she was anyway.

They had been robbed.

CHAPTER 48

With Kim and Joe covering and tackling like demons in defence, and Craig playing well in goal, Atlantis managed to keep the scoreline to 1-0 at half-time, when they sat down in a circle on the field to recover their breath and their energy.

As they sipped cold drinks they complained bitterly about the refereeing.

'Where did they get him from?' asked Craig.

'He's a local, a Brazilian,' said Ajit.

'He seems to be able to chat away to all their team anyway,' said Kim.

'I suppose they could be from Portugal,' suggested Ajit.

'Or Brazil?' said Craig.

'So that's why they didn't need to acclimatise to this humidity. They're all locals,' said Kim.

Ajit and Jess's faces fell, but the rest of the players just looked angry.

'Look, there's no point complaining about that,' said Joe.

'Leave that to Victor and his brother to sort out.

'We have to go out and try to equalise, and then go for the winner. And they're not that good. The Barcelona guy is flashy, but he's soft too. Every time he gets the ball Ajit and I will sandwich him. Just keep fighting hard, we'll get there. Let's start this half like a train and try to catch them cold. But be careful, I reckon the first person to even look at the ref without smiling will get a red card.'

The referee whistled to get the second half under way and immediately the Atlanteans went on the attack. The Hy-Brasilians had been laughing and joking at half-time and seemed to be a little complacent about their opponents.

Joe waltzed past his cover and flicked the ball out to Ajit who ran as far as the goal line before turning and looping a cross into the penalty area. The Atlantis captain raced towards where he thought the ball would arrive, and as he leapt in the air he remembered back to the videos of Ronaldo they had watched. He tried to copy the way the star moved in the air and hung there for half a moment, arching his neck and shoulders and meeting the ball with his full forehead.

The ball cannoned off his head and buried itself in the net

with the goalkeeper standing open-mouthed as the youngster ran away with his arm in the air.

The Atlantis staff let loose a roar of delight and with the referee unable to see anything wrong with the goal, he whistled weakly and pointed to half-way.

Hy-Brasil were angry and turned up the heat for the next few minutes, but Craig was inspired between the goalposts. He dived full-length to save the ball from one vicious curling shot by the sole female on the visiting team and blocked the rebound when the full-back came racing through.

But the Hy-Brasilians seemed to grow bored with their efforts. They were certainly having no problems with stamina, but just seemed less interested in the result than Joe and his pals were.

Joe looked across at Kalvin, who urged him to get forward. Atlantis were awarded a free on the edge of their own area and Joe took a breather while he studied his choices. He signalled to Kim and glanced across at Ajit and indicated with his eyes what he wanted him to do.

Joe played the ball back to Kim, and then set off on a charge up field on his own. The Hy-Brasil defence was startled, and took their eyes off Kim, who had passed the ball out to Ajit who was haring down the wing. Joe reached the penalty spot, around where he scored with the header, but this time two Hy-Brasil backs had him covered so he ducked when the cross came in.

The ball ran across to Jess who took half a second to control the ball before firing it at near post where the ball sneaked between the goalkeeper and the upright into the net.

There was an even louder cheer from the Atlantis supporters, and Joe smiled as he saw the referee shrug his shoulders as if to say, 'what can I do?' and signal that he had awarded the goal.

The yellow shirts seemed to wake up and realise they were now 2-1 down, but try as they might they couldn't find their way through. Even little Jess tore into tackles, and even won one as the Hy-Brasil star player soon lost heart.

The visitor's only girl, Marta, was not so soft however, and she kept rallying her team to find an equaliser.

With just a few seconds left on the clock she broke past Joe and zeroed in on goal. Kim moved across to cut her off, but Marta wriggled past her and got a shot in. It flew like an arrow from her boot and was bound for the top right-hand corner of the goal.

Craig, however, had other plans for the ball. Drawing on everything he had learned in gymnastics class, he dived high in the air and flung his arms at the ball as it was just under the crossbar – and the top fingertip of his glove connected enough to send the ball off course and hit the woodwork. It bounced down towards Marta who swung hard but kicked under the ball and it flew high over the bar and over the fence into the river.

The Hy-Brasil player looked to the sideline, but no spare ball seemed to be available, so she rushed to the door in the fence and opened it.

'NO!' called Luce from the sideline, but among the cheers for the save her voice went unheard.

Marta knelt on the side of the island and leaned out towards the ball, which had drifted back within a metre of dry land. Her fingers brushed the leather before she felt two strong arms hauling her back from the river.

'No, no, no,' said Craig, as he wrestled her away from the water.

'What's happening?' asked Ajit.

'I don't know,' said Joe. 'Craig seems to have gone mad.'

The referee rushed to the fence and waved a red card at Craig.

But the goalkeeper pointed at the ball, which was already starting to change shape as the air leaked out.

'Look!'

The ball was suddenly covered in small fish, which leapt out of the water to snap away at the leather. Within seconds it was in shreds, ripped into a million pieces by small, vicious teeth.

CHAPTER 49

'**P**iranha!' screamed the referee, terrified at the Amazonian fish who the legend says can reduce a man to a skeleton in minutes.

The official blew his whistle and rushed everyone back inside the fence. He called Aston and Victor into the middle and they had a short conversation in Portuguese. Victor walked across to the children.

'He says he has to abandon the match because the match ball has been destroyed, which I told him is utter nonsense. There were ten seconds to go and it was a goal-kick to Atlantis. I've asked Aston to talk to him.'

But Aston wasn't talking to the referee – he was involved in a heated discussion with Kratos. After a minute or two he walked over to the Atlantis team followed by his partner.

'Kratos won't budge,' he began, before steeling himself. 'But this is my bet and even though Kratos recruited these star players this team is playing in my name. And I concede victory to a brave and superior side.'

Kratos snarled at Aston. 'This is bull,' he said. 'You won't hear the end of this,' and stormed off.

The referee signalled to Craig to take the goal-kick, but four of the Hy-Brasil team had also walked off the field, so Joe and Kim just kicked the ball back and forth to each other until the final whistle sounded seconds later.

The five Atlanteans hugged each other with delight, and their supporters rushed on to congratulate them. Marta waited to shake each of them by the hand, but the rest of the Hy-Brasil team were already in their dinghy and heading back to their island.

'You played very well,' Marta told Joe. 'But you know we are not students of this island – we all come from the academies of big Brazilian clubs. There are five other kids over there who they have hidden away.'

Joe nodded and thanked her for being honest.

Marta blushed, and whispered in Joe's ear. 'And we had a video of your training sessions and all your moves. The ref was definitely crooked too. He has been banned in Brazil for two years for taking bribes. You had no chance and you still won.'

And with that Marta jumped into another dinghy and

waited for the last of the Hy-Brasil entourage to join her.

Joe and Kim walked up to where Luce and Kalvin were both wearing smiles as wide as a watermelon. Joe shocked them by filling them in on what Marta had told her about the referee, and how none of her team were students on Hy-Brasil, and how they had worked out all Atlantis's tactics in advance.

Victor and Aston were still involved in an intense conversation which only ended with Victor storming away looking very annoyed and Aston making sheepishly for the last dinghy.

With the last of the visitors gone, and Hy-Brasil submerged, the winning team and coaches sat on the grassy hill and looked down on their field of victory. Luce served soft drinks and juice for the kids, and the adults toasted their success with champagne. Kalvin brought out two large lamps and a barbecue and helped Maureen to cook a celebratory feast.

'What a glorious day that was,' said Luce as they watched the sun go down behind the canopy of the Amazonian jungle.

They all laughed and joked as they munched on their

meal – Craig even tried a barbecued piranha – and relived every moment of the game.

Victor came back upstairs to join them, this time wearing his smartest white suit. 'I always dress up for parties,' he told them.

Luce smiled, and asked him was he relieved to have won the bet and saved Atlantis.

'Of course I am,' he replied, 'and I feel very foolish to have come so close to losing it.'

'And now you have a second island to take care of. That should be quite a challenge,' Luce noted.

'Well… that will not be the case,' sighed Victor. 'Aston is not a bad man, just a weak one. He confessed to me at the end there that he actually only owns one per cent of Hy-Brasil. Kratos had bought him out years ago. He led me to believe he owned it all – so I risked losing Atlantis against gaining just a tiny piece of his academy.'

The Atlantis staff were so stunned nobody could say anything.

'And that of course means we still have Kratos dogging our every move and continuing to cheat their way to sporting success.'

'But that's not your way,' said Kim. 'And it's not our way either.'

They all sat down and toasted Craig and the crucial extra two centimetres he had grown that saved the day. And they laughed and sang and ate and drank long into the night on their Amazon island, enjoying each other and the camaraderie of being a team united.

Atlantis United.

TURN THE PAGE FOR A SNEAK PEEK

AT THE NEXT GREAT

SPORTS ACADEMY ADVENTURE

CHAPTER 1

Whenever Kim couldn't sleep she went for a long walk. Living on a submarine, that wasn't as easy as it might sound, but Kim had a good imagination.

Creeping past her roommate's bed, Kim grinned as she listened to the snorts and whistles made by Jess – and made a mental note to record them and play them back to her some morning. As silently as possible, she let herself out of the room and headed down the corridor.

The submarine, which was disguised as a small island, purred gently as it travelled through the ocean. Kim didn't have much of an idea where they were, preferring to leave all that to the captain, and Luce, who ran the Atlantis Academy.

Kim had been selected for the sports programme some months before, despite being a very ordinary performer on her primary school rugby team. The rest of the kids were just as bad at their favourite sports, but all shared a determination and willingness to get better.

So far, the students had all shown huge improvements, especially in football where they had a brilliant, eccentric coach to inspire them, and had helped Atlantis win a crucial match deep in the jungles of South America.

Kim wandered through the school till she found her favourite room, the sporting simulator. It was here they could practise by taking penalties against the best goalkeeper in the world, or even play a game of tennis against a hologram of a legendary player. Kim liked to go for walks but found it boring doing so around the gloomy corridors, so she came up with a brilliant plan – she slowed a running machine down to a gentle pace and adjusted the video pictures that bathed the room so it showed a golf course, or the route of every Olympic marathon race.

'I think I'd like to see what Beijing looks like at this time of year,' she chuckled to herself, as she hopped onto the walking machine.

It wasn't easy to find space to keep to yourself on a submarine, and Kim enjoyed it whenever she could get it, even if it was at the cost of sleep. She always loved walks in the countryside to relax back at home, but this was a different type of exercise, and she found it interesting to see how people lived in other countries. She hadn't travelled much before her Atlantis adventure had begun and even since they had very little taste of the places they had visited. She hoped that would change.

She was really getting into her walk, even waving at some of the people she passed on her journey around the Chinese city, when a knock came to the door. In walked Kelly, the talent scout who had invited Kim to Atlantis Academy.

'Hi, Kim,' she said, with a big grin. 'Great to see you, even at this ridiculous hour.'

'Wow, hi, Kelly,' frowned Kim as she checked her watch and saw that it was 3am.

'Are you finding it hard to sleep too? This is my first night on board and I can't get used to the movement.'

'It's not bad after a while, I just can't sleep when Jess is snoring,' Kim said, smiling.

Kelly laughed. 'Great to see you using the machines so creatively, I was watching you on the monitors up in the control room.'

'Really? They can see us up there?' replied Kim, blushing. 'Waving at the crowds and all?'

'Well, yes, I suppose they have to keep tabs on where

everyone is.'

'So, when did you arrive?' asked Kim, changing the subject.

'Last night, about ten o'clock,' said Kelly. 'I flew to Boston and then took a little boat out into the Atlantic with one of Kalvin's friends. The island came to the surface and I hopped on board. I wasn't surprised there wasn't a welcoming party. It was verrrrrrry cold.'

'And why did you come?'

'Oh, sorry, have they not explained? We're on the second phase of your training now. You're going to the Rugby World Cup.'

CHAPTER 2

Back in her bed, Kim tried hard to sleep but Kelly's arrival had just given her brain more to buzz about. She had really enjoyed learning and playing football, but rugby was the sport that she loved the most.

Her dad had been a good player back home, but too many injuries forced him to give it up before she was born. She loved going to watch games with him and meeting his old friends, but one day he got sick and soon afterwards stopped going. Life got harder for Kim and her little brother; their mum was hardly around after she had to take up a second job.

Then one day Kim saw a poster in school asking for girls to join a new rugby team so she put her name down. She wasn't very good, but she knew all the laws and had loads of good ideas and tips which helped her friends. Her dad started coming along to watch their games, and even their training sessions.

'This is such a tonic for your father,' her mum confided in

her one day. 'Since he got sick he hasn't had much interest in anything, but your rugby has been a great boost to him.'

Kim couldn't wait to find out more about the World Cup so she could tell him on the next of the monthly video phone calls they were permitted. Although she hadn't even held a rugby ball since she arrived on Atlantis she knew that all the training and fitness work had made her a better player.

It felt like she had been asleep for five minutes when the alarm clock rang, and Jess sprang up out of her bed on the other side of the room.

'Good morning, Kimmy!' she called, sounding far more energetic and enthusiastic than Kim felt.

'Uhhhhhhmmmnggg,' she grunted in reply.

Kim lifted her legs off the bed slowly, one by one. She buried her face in her hands and tried to rub the sleep out of her eyes. She loved Jess – everyone did – but she could be a little giddy just when you didn't want her to be.

'You look wretched, Kimmy,' said Jess.

'I didn't sleep well,' she replied, 'I even went for a walk to try to tire myself out but that was interrupted.' She explained about Kelly and her news.

'Wow! A World Cup? That will be awesome, I wonder when we're going to learn how to play this sport though...'

Kim laughed, and then went white. 'Oh no... of course... I'm the only one who's ever played rugby before!'

That wasn't quite true, she discovered over breakfast with the rest of her classmates.

'I joined a club last winter,' explained Craig. 'We had a really horrible coach though, so I gave up after three or four sessions. I really enjoyed playing though and love watching it on TV.'

Craig had joined the Academy as a tennis player, but like all the kids he was expected to throw himself into every sport that was offered to him. Jess was mainly an athlete, while Ajit had been picked because of one flash of magic he'd shown when using his cricket skills in a hurling match. Joe had been the worst footballer on his club team, but he loved the sport and was willing to work hard to improve and the scout valued that most of all. He was recruited by Atlantis Academy and captained the football team to victory in that high-stakes match in Brazil.

'Yeah, the Six Nations is always great to watch,' agreed Joe. 'But it sometimes looks very rough…'

Joe's comment was interrupted by the arrival of Kelly, who asked could she join them.

'Let me guess, Joe,' she smiled. 'You're not talking about the table tennis tournament this morning?'

Joe grinned back at her. 'Ah no, I wouldn't mind playing rugby at all,' he said. 'It's just some of those forwards are HUGE, and when they run into you it must hurt a lot.'

'Well, yes, the adult game can be very physical, but when you're playing against people your own size it's a lot less harmful. But we'll train you all to do the right things and how to avoid damaging yourself or your opponent.'

'Tell us more about this World Cup,' asked Jess.

'Well…' Kelly started, 'I'm not sure how much I can say yet. But it's a special World Cup for kids that will be run alongside the main one in Japan. You'll be meeting lots of kids from all over the world, representing countries, schools, clubs – and independent island academies…'

'You mean besides us? Not that horrible one in Brazil?' asked Jess.

'No…' said Kelly. 'We're not the only school like this, you know. Although we are the only one that works like a submarine.'

'Japan!' said Craig. 'Wow, I've always wanted to go there…'

Ajit looked a bit concerned though. He stirred his smoothie and looked at Kelly.

'Hang on,' he started. 'Is it a five-a-side rugby competition? How does that work?'

'Ah… No,' replied Kelly. 'It will be Sevens… which means we're going to have to get you some new team-mates.'